Ju
F
P47   Pfeffer, Susan.
              Turning thirteen.

DATE   ISSU...

Ju
F
P47   Pfeffer, Susan.
           Turning thirteen.

Temple Israel Library
Minneapolis, Minn.

———

Please sign your full name on the above card.

Return books promptly to the Library or Temple Office.

Fines will be charged for overdue books or for damage or loss of same.

TURNING THIRTEEN

Also by
SUSAN BETH PFEFFER

The Friendship Pact
Truth or Dare
Starting with Melodie
Kid Power Strikes Back
Kid Power

TURNING THIRTEEN

Susan Beth Pfeffer

SCHOLASTIC
HARDCOVER

Scholastic Inc.
New York

Library of Congress Cataloging-in-Publication Data

Pfeffer, Susan Beth, 1948-
    Turning thirteen.

    Summary: Although initially afraid that she'll lose her best friend unless
they prepare for their bat mitzvahs together, Becky undergoes a change in
her thinking that puts much more than her friendship in jeopardy.
    [1. Bat mitzvah—Fiction. 2. Friendship—Fiction]
I. Title.
PZ7.P44855Tu   1988   [Fic]   88-11347
ISBN 0-590-40764-3

12 11 10 9 8 7 6 5 4 3 2 1   8 9/8 0 1 2 3/9

                    Printed in the U.S.A.   12

            First Scholastic printing, October 1988

For Bill Soiffer and Jacquie Sweeny-Soiffer

Useful Terms

Bar mitzvah — A boy's confirmation

Bat mitzvah — A girl's confirmation

Haftorah — Readings from the Books of the Prophets

Kiddush — A gathering with drinking of wine to celebrate a joyous religious event

Kosher — Biblical rules governing what you may eat

Sh'ma — A prayer saying God is One

Torah — The first five books of the Bible

One

According to the clock over the door, there was one minute and forty-seven seconds left before the bell was going to ring, and I was spending every one of those seconds in prayer.

Dear God, please don't let her call on me.

Mrs. Maguire, my social studies teacher, was going around the room asking us the names of the state capitals. I'd meant to memorize them the night before, but I started reading a book instead and never got around to it. When you're trying to figure out who stole the missing purloined manuscript faster than the heroine does, memorizing capitals just isn't something you think to do. And the heroine had a headstart on me anyway, knowing what "purloined" meant. I kept thinking it was a cut of beef.

So I prayed hard. Prayer didn't always work, but there was no harm in trying it. I attempted to feel spiritual but look knowledgeable. If Mrs. Maguire figured out I was praying, she'd know for sure I hadn't memorized the capitals and she'd skip order and go straight for me. Mrs. Maguire had killer instincts.

"The capital of New Jersey is Trenton."

I looked over at Amy Ford. She had the look of a girl who knew all her capitals. I hated her. Not that I had much liked her before we started this capital business. Amy Ford was one of those perfect people you sometimes meet. She always knew the answers, she dressed wonderfully, she was kind to old ladies and cats, and worst of all, my best friend of forever, Dina Cohen, was starting to like her a little too much.

Please, God, don't let Mrs. Maguire reach me.

Up until that day, I hadn't spent much time thinking about God. He was just up there, answering prayers, knowing everything, doing God business. I saw a movie once where George Burns played Him, but that wasn't the way I pictured God at all. He looked more like my great-grandfather, big, with a beard, and He spoke with a Russian accent. Somehow I was sure God had an accent. After all, it was pretty presumptuous to think He came from America.

If Mrs. Maguire doesn't call on me, I promise I'll memorize all the state capitals the minute I get home, God.

"The capital of California is Sacramento."

I had thought Sacramento was some kind of

tomato juice, but then again, I'd kept waiting for them to cut a piece of manuscript last night and barbecue it. I knew I should have memorized those stupid state capitals. You never knew when a state capital would come in handy. There were probably people out there who knew every state capital and recited them for a living. I'd hire one on the spot if I could.

I looked at Dina. She'd gone twelve state capitals ago, telling everyone that the capital of Maine was Augusta. Dina always did better at school than I did. My mother says Dina isn't any smarter than I am, and if I want to do as well I should just study more, but there are so many other more interesting things to do than memorize state capitals. Of course Dina found the time to do the interesting stuff as well as her schoolwork, and I never seemed to be able to. Then again, Dina probably couldn't have figured out that Andrew Dare, the no-good nephew, was behind the stolen purloined manuscript.

"Different people have different talents," my mother always says.

Dear God, if Mrs. Maguire doesn't reach me, I promise I'll use my talents for the good of humanity.

I thought about that prayer for a moment. It seemed to be offering a lot for very little. Then again, I didn't know what my talents were, so it probably didn't matter. Unless it meant I'd just sworn I was going to become a detective. Not that I'd mind being a detective. I just wasn't sure I wanted to commit to it because I hadn't memorized state capitals. You never knew what God was going to hold you to.

"The capital of Idaho is Boise."

I was impressed. It seemed like everyone in the room had memorized those capitals except me. I waited for the next state capital to be Girlse, but it wasn't. It turned out the capital of Virginia was Richmond. These kids were smart. Either that, or they'd prayed just the right way before getting called.

Dear God, if Mrs. Maguire gets to me, how about if she asks me a capital I know?

I figured I must know a capital or two. I'd sort of looked at the list the night before, and maybe I had memorized them without really knowing I had. Or God could just float the answer into my brain like a miracle. God was great on miracles, and this one, as miracles went, shouldn't take too much effort on His part.

"The capital of Arkansas is Little Rock."

That was a killer. It was bad enough that there were fifty states and fifty capitals. There was no reason why some of those capitals had to have two-word names.

I looked again at Dina, hoping she'd see me and smile and send me some capitals by wavelength. Dina and I used to think the same thoughts all the time. I'd start to say something and she'd finish it before half the words were out of my mouth. That's how it is with best friends. And Dina and I were even closer than best friends. We were practically sisters, the way I saw it. The way Dina used to see it, too.

"The capital of Wyoming is Cheyenne."

I thought Johnny Mulligan had said Shy Anne and I laughed at his mistake. No one else laughed. I knew I was in deep trouble.

Dear God, please don't have Mrs. Maguire care that I laughed.

"Becky, what is the capital of Washington?"

This was completely unfair. I wasn't supposed to go for another capital. Now God had no time to send the answer to me, and there were still a good thirty seconds before the bell was going to ring.

"Excuse me?" I said, to give God and the wavelengths an extra few seconds.

"The capital of Washington, Becky," Mrs. Maguire said.

"The capital of Washington is D.C.," I said.

Everyone laughed then, except for Mrs. Maguire. Even Dina was laughing. And Amy was smiling politely. I sincerely wished I was dead so I could go to heaven and give God a piece of my mind.

"Becky, have you learned any of the state capitals?" Mrs. Maguire asked.

"Sure," I said. "The capital of Iowa is Girlse. No, I mean Wyoming. Boise. No, that's Shy Amy. No, I mean Anne."

Mrs. Maguire's jaw dropped a good six inches. Her chin practically reached her waist. Everyone else was roaring with laughter. Even Amy had given up being polite and was whooping it up with the rest of them. I just sat there and wished God would strike them all down dead. The way I saw it, He owed me a big one.

So, of course, then the bell rang. The bell always rings a minute too late. I wondered if it was that way for everyone, or if God had decided to pick on me and me alone.

"Very well, class," Mrs. Maguire said. "You may all go, except for Becky Weiss."

Big surprise. Everybody else got their books together and started trooping out of the classroom. Dina, I saw, waited for Amy, and the two of them walked out together. I sat absolutely still in my chair and thought about how I wasn't going to cry.

When the classroom was finally empty, Mrs. Maguire stood with her back to her desk, stared straight at me, and said, "Now, Becky, what are we going to do with you?"

I don't like Mrs. Maguire. She's boring and she makes fun of kids she doesn't like, and I bet every night before she falls asleep she recites all the state capitals in alphabetical order. Some nights she probably does it in reverse alphabetical order for excitement.

The problem was Mrs. Maguire doesn't like me, either. And she's the teacher and I'm the kid and those are lousy odds.

"I'm sorry," I muttered. Sometimes apologizing helps.

"I'm sure you are," Mrs. Maguire declared. "Sorry about what, Becky?"

6

"That I didn't know the capital of Washington," I said. "Are you sure it isn't D.C.?"

"I'm sure," Mrs. Maguire said. She continued to stare at me and sighed. I sighed back. Probably somewhere up in heaven, God was sighing right along with us.

"When you were in school, did you ever pray?" I asked Mrs. Maguire. My father says that in negotiations it helps to understand your opponent.

"That is none of your business," Mrs. Maguire replied.

"Oh," I said.

"I don't know where you learned your manners, but you can be the rudest child I've ever met," Mrs. Maguire declared. "Polite people never discuss religion."

"I didn't know that," I said.

"There's a lot you don't know," Mrs. Maguire said. "Starting with the state capitals."

"I really do know some of them," I said. "I just got confused."

"Very well, then," she said. "What is the capital of Nebraska?"

I closed my eyes and tried hard to remember what that list of capitals had looked like. I could picture the list, but the words on it kept shifting out of focus.

"I don't know," I admitted.

"The capital of Florida?"

"I don't know."

"The capital of Ohio?"

I shook my head and prayed I wouldn't cry.

"You don't know any of the capitals, do you?" Mrs. Maguire said.

"The capital of New York is Albany," I said. "I know that one."

"We live in New York," Mrs. Maguire said. "I should hope you would know its state capital."

"I've been there," I said. "My family went there once."

"I'm sure that's very interesting," Mrs. Maguire said. "But it's hardly relevant. Becky, I gave you a homework assignment and you failed to do it. I know you're capable of memorizing all the state capitals. You were just too lazy to bother."

"I wasn't lazy," I said. "I was reading a book."

"Reading is fine, but there's more to life than books," Mrs. Maguire said. "There's homework and coming to class prepared. And that's where you failed. You do admit you failed, don't you Becky?"

I nodded.

"And that you were rude?"

"I didn't mean to be rude," I said.

"No one means to be rude," Mrs. Maguire said. "But rudeness is wrong, just as coming unprepared is."

I wondered if it was rude of me to ask God to strike Mrs. Maguire down dead immediately and painfully. It didn't matter. God was not exactly coming through for me that afternoon.

"Very well," Mrs. Maguire said. "Tomorrow I expect you to know all your state capitals, Becky. I will keep you after school and have you recite each and every one of them to me."

"All right," I said, starting to get my books.

"Wait one second, young lady," Mrs. Maguire said. "I never said I was through with you."

So I sat still again.

"I also expect you to write out each state and its capital three times," she declared. "In full sentences. 'The capital of Alabama is Montgomery. The capital of Alaska is Juneau.' Do you understand?"

"I understand."

"I also want you to write the sentence, 'It is rude to discuss religion' twenty-five times," Mrs. Maguire said. "Are you writing all this down?"

Mrs. Maguire knew perfectly well I wasn't writing all this down. I was sitting right in front of her, obviously not writing. I frowned, got out my assignment book and a pencil, and wrote, "It is rude to discuss religion twenty-five times," just to make her happy.

"And I want those lists handwritten," Mrs. Maguire said. "Don't write them out on a computer or think you can make one list and then get it photocopied. Every single word must be written by you in longhand. And neatness counts."

I nodded. Neatness always did.

"If you don't have all the capitals memorized by tomorrow, and the lists of capitals neatly written out, and the sentence 'It is rude to discuss religion' written out twenty-five times, I will have to write a note to your parents," Mrs. Maguire said. "So that they can deal with you as well."

My parents hate it when my teachers are mad at me. I hate it when my parents are mad at me. If I'd had any doubts about state capitals before then, they were gone. "I promise I'll do it," I said. "Please don't write my parents."

"Very well, Becky," Mrs. Maguire said. "You do realize that these extra assignments don't excuse you from doing your regular homework."

"I'll do everything," I said. "May I please be excused now?"

"After you apologize to me," she said. "For forcing me to stay late to talk with you."

"I'm sorry I forced you to stay late to talk with me," I said. I meant it, too. "Now may I go?"

"Very well," Mrs. Maguire said. "But I expect to see a different attitude from you tomorrow."

"Thank you," I said. I swallowed hard, grabbed my books, and got out of there as fast as possible. None of it was fair. Just because of a few lousy seconds, I had to write all those dumb lists over and over again and apologize to Mrs. Maguire and live in constant fear that she would tell my parents just what she thought of me. And I'd been stuck after school so long, there was no way Dina would be waiting for me.

Except there she was, right by the willow tree! I couldn't believe it. Of course it used to be I would have automatically known Dina would be waiting, but now with this Amy Ford in our school, half the time Dina went off with her somewhere and forgot all about me. But not today. True friendships really count. I ran right over to the willow tree, feeling better than I thought I ever would again.

"Dina!" I shouted. "Thanks for waiting."

"Amy thought we should," Dina replied.

I looked around, and sure enough, there was Amy. "Was she awful?" Amy asked.

Not as awful as you are, I thought. "She was okay," I said. "She said I was rude a lot."

"I don't think you're rude," Amy said politely. Amy has manners like that. If she were burning on fire, she'd probably say "excuse me" to the fire-fighters.

"Becky's rude," Dina said. "You just don't know her well enough to know that, Amy."

"Dina and I have been best friends forever," I told Amy. "Since before we were born."

"Becky," Dina said.

"Our parents met at Lamaze classes," I informed Amy. "They all breathed together. Dina was born four days before me. Then her mother and mine went to the same La Leche League meetings together. So we nursed together, too. Naturally, we're best friends."

"Naturally," Amy said. "I wish I had a best friend I'd known my whole life."

"We've known each other even longer than that," I boasted. "My mother helped Dina's mother pick her name."

"I wish she'd picked something different," Dina said. "Come on, Amy, let's go. We were just waiting to make sure you were okay, Becky. See you tomorrow."

"But Dina," I said, only it didn't matter. Dina had turned her back on me and she and Amy were whispering and walking away. Whispering something about me, I figured. Something about how dumb I was.

God, please let Dina be my best friend again.

I stared at the blue sky, where God was probably hanging out, and then I started the lonely walk home.

Two

How did the audit go?" Dad asked Mom as we sat around the dinner table that evening.

"Don't ask," Mom replied. "Danny, could you pass me the string beans?"

"Sure," Danny said, and sent them along. Danny is three years older than me. He hates string beans, so it was no sacrifice for him to get rid of them. I was disappointed, though. His elbow kept hovering around the bowl, and I was waiting to see if he'd ever end up with his arm covered by beans.

"They weren't cooperative?" Dad asked. I guess he figured "don't ask" meant "keep on asking."

"More like hostile," Mom said, helping herself to the beans. "I never understand these firms. They call me in specifically because they need help, and then the moment I enter the door, it's obstruction and misdirection and delay. And then they blame me for taking too long."

"You could always quit," Danny said.

"I love being an accountant," Mom declared. "Most of the time."

"The chicken's very good tonight," Dad said. "New recipe?"

"Becky was a big help," Mom said. "She had half the dinner ready before I even got home."

I smiled modestly. It had seemed to me helping out with supper wouldn't hurt if somehow Mom and Dad found out about my afternoon problems with state capitals. There was no reason why they should know, unless I told them, which I certainly wasn't about to, but parents have natural gifts for learning just what you don't want them to know. So I was unusually helpful when I got home from school. But not so helpful that it would be obvious I was in trouble. Not that I was in that much trouble. Just a little bit of helpfulness for a little bit of trouble. By the time you're twelve, you know how to measure these things.

"So how was your school day, Danny?" Dad asked. "Did you get your English test back?"

"I got a ninety-two," Danny replied. "And Mr. Edwards wrote 'good job' on the essay part."

"That's great," Dad said. "I know how hard you studied for it. Anything else exciting happen?"

"I did a proof on the chalkboard in geometry," Danny replied. "I didn't think I was going to get it, but I did. And in French, I did a translation out loud and got most of it. There were a couple of words I had trouble with but Madame Steinmetz didn't mind. She just told me to guess, so I did, and I got one of the words right from the context. She said to do that — think about what the paragraph was about, and then if you don't know the actual word, see if you can work it out based on the context."

"Very good," Mom said. "How was your day, Becky?"

I no longer remembered. All I could think of was state capitals, and that was the last thing I cared to discuss that evening. "Is it wrong to talk about religion?" I asked instead.

"How do you mean 'wrong'?" Dad asked. "For that matter, how do you mean 'talk about'?"

"I don't know," I said. "Just 'talk about.' Mrs. Maguire said it was rude to talk about religion, and I was wondering if it was."

"It's certainly rude to insult someone else's religion," Mom declared. "You can't say your religion is better than someone else's. But I don't think it's rude to ask questions, provided you word them politely."

"That's what I thought," I said. "Thanks."

"Some people think it's rude, though," Dad said. "My mother for one. She always says, 'Never talk about religion or politics.'"

"But Granny talks about religion and politics all the time," I pointed out. "Whenever we see her, we always get into fights about religion and politics."

"Those aren't fights, they're heated discussions," Mom said. "Granny likes to discuss things heatedly."

15

"Well, whatever they are, they're about religion and politics," I said.

"But she only discusses them with family," Dad declared. "With family you can pretty much discuss anything. Although even there, you shouldn't act superior."

"Uncle Bob acts superior," Danny said. "Ever since he got religious, he acts superior all the time. He won't even eat here anymore because we don't keep kosher."

"He'll get over it," Mom said.

"Being religious?" I asked. "Do you get over that?"

"Being superior," Mom replied. "When you first fall in love with anything, a person or an idea, that becomes the be-all and the end-all in your life. Then, after a while, you adjust, and you regain your perspective. Bob's in love with Judaism right now. In a few months, he won't be any less in love, but he'll be more adjusted to it, and he'll start talking about other things."

"I sure hope so," Dad grumbled.

"Me, too," Danny said. "When we were over at his house last week, all he kept asking me was did I still go to synagogue? Did I pray every day?"

I'd prayed enough today to satisfy even Uncle Bob, but I didn't say so. Besides, I had the feeling Uncle Bob wanted more grateful kinds of prayers.

"I'm glad for Bob," Mom said. "In the sixties, he really got involved in things, organizing anti-war rallies and sit-ins. And nothing's replaced that

16

for him until now. I'm glad he has something to commit to."

"He wouldn't if it weren't for what's-her-face, Judy," Dad declared. "If Judy weren't religious, and Bob weren't so hot for her, none of this religion business would have happened."

"He wouldn't have fallen for a woman like Judy if he didn't feel the need for something more in his life," Mom replied. "You never did understand Bob."

"Of course I understand Bob," Dad replied. "I just don't understand why he has to get Orthodox on us like this. And he keeps changing the rules. One week it's okay for us to call him on Saturday. The next week he announces he's observing the Sabbath completely, no phone calls, no driving. It kills Saturday for me. We used to play tennis on Saturdays and now he won't and I resent that."

"It wouldn't hurt if we all observed the Sabbath just a little more," Mom declared. "When was the last time you went to temple, Hal?"

"Fairly recently," Dad said, but he looked uncomfortable. "All right, Annie, when did I go to temple last?"

"For the High Holy Days," Mom replied. "And that was the only time you went all year except for Alex Siegel's bar mitzvah."

"Boy, that was some affair," Dad said. "They had ice sculptures in the shape of Sid and Helen Siegel's faces."

"They paid for the bar mitzvah party, they wanted

to show off," Mom said. "But that's beside the point."

"Come on, now, it was pretty funny watching Helen Siegel's face melt," Dad said. He carved off a little piece of chicken and nibbled on it.

"Her nose went first," Mom said, and she giggled at the memory. "It was like watching a nose job in progress."

"We didn't have any ice sculptures at my bar mitzvah party, did we?" Danny asked.

"Your grandparents were too cheap for that," Dad replied. "A little chopped liver, a half pound of pastrami, that's all they sprung for."

"Good," Danny said.

"You were there," I said. "Don't you remember what the party was like?"

Danny shook his head. "I mostly hung out with my friends," he said. "And checked out the loot I was getting."

"Great," Mom said. "Bob has the right idea. Religion isn't supposed to be about loot and ice sculptures. It's about your relationship with God."

Right then my relationship with God could have used some work, but I wasn't about to say so. One wrong comment and my relationship with my parents would also be in trouble.

"Bob's religion has a lot more to do with his relationship with Judy," Dad declared. "I hope they'll be very happy together, but I wish he'd start playing tennis on Saturdays again."

"I think we should all go to temple together on

Saturday," Mom said. "The way we used to when the kids were little."

"I really have to work this Saturday," Dad said. "I have a lot to catch up on at the office."

"But the Sabbath is for resting," Mom said.

"Then God should have created an eight-day week," Dad replied. "The Henderson Chemical brief is due on Tuesday, and I'll be working straight through the weekend."

"Then the kids and I will go," Mom said.

"I can't," Danny said.

"Do I have to?" I said.

Mom would have killed one of us, except the phone rang. We all jumped up to answer it, but Mom was closest so she got there first.

"One of you should go to temple with her," Dad whispered while Mom was away. "Let her get it out of her system. Come on, Becky. One Saturday for a little bit of peace."

"Right, Becky," Danny said. "Besides, this is all your fault. You were the one who brought up religion in the first place."

"But it's boring," I said. "All you do is pray and sing songs and listen to the stupid sermon."

"That's what religion is all about," Dad replied. "Praying and singing and listening. I don't say you should go every week, but once in a while, for the sake of a little family unity, isn't such a bad idea."

"I don't see why I have to go," I grumbled. "Why can't Danny go instead? I helped make supper."

"There's a football game Saturday," Danny said. "The band has to be there by eleven."

"It's not fair," I said. "Why do I have to go when it's Mom's idea?"

"Because you love her and want to make her happy," Dad replied.

I scowled. "You love her and want to make her happy, too," I said. "But you're not going."

"You want to write the Henderson brief, fine," Dad said. "If between now and Saturday you can go to law school, get your degree, pass the bar exam, and get hired by my law firm, I'll go to temple and let you write the brief."

There were some distinct disadvantages to being the youngest. But even if I were Danny's age, the odds were I couldn't get all that done by Saturday.

"Don't worry," Danny said. "By Saturday, Mom may have forgotten all about it. She gets these religious spells sometimes, but they always go away real fast."

"I'll tell you what," Dad said. "If Mom doesn't mention it again, I won't bring it up, either."

"Okay," I muttered. This had been one terrible day, and with the way things were going, that was the best deal I could hope for.

We could hear Mom say good-bye and hang up the phone. She came back into the dining room and sat down. "Talk about coincidences," she said. "That was Becky's teacher."

"Mrs. Maguire?" I squeaked. The already bad day was threatening to become the worst day of my life.

"No, Mrs. Levinson from Hebrew School," Mom

replied. "She wanted to know what we'd decided about Becky's bat mitzvah."

"I didn't know we'd decided anything," Dad said.

"Neither did I," Mom said. "I told Mrs. Levinson I thought girls had their bat mitzvahs at twelve, and since Becky's been twelve for several months now, we must have decided not to have one. Only she said at our temple, the girls have it at thirteen, same as the boys. They do the same exact things as the boys — read from the Torah and the Haftorah, and conduct services, everything, and it takes about six months of study, same as it was for Danny, and was Becky interested in becoming a bat mitzvah?"

"It's a lot of work," Danny said. "But you get good money and lots of gifts."

"And it's a nice opportunity to show off," Dad said. "You're the center of attention that day. Plus there's a party. For you we'll have ice sculptures."

"Wait a second," I said. "What if I don't want to?"

"Then you don't have to," Mom replied. "It's not required. But it is a wonderful chance to participate in Judaism. When I was a girl, a bat mitzvah wasn't such a big deal. It was just kind of a throwaway so you wouldn't get too jealous of the fuss being made over the boys. I went to some bar mitzvah parties that cost a fortune. But nowadays, in Reform and Conservative Judaism, a bat mitzvah is a real religious event."

"But six months of studying," I said. "I'd still have to go to school, too." The thought of memorizing all the state capitals *plus* a lot of prayers in Hebrew was definitely depressing.

"It's your decision," Dad said. "But if you decide to do it, we'll help you any way we can. Plus give you a big party."

"Why are you so enthusiastic about the idea?" Mom asked.

"I want to rub Bob's nose in it," Dad declared. "Six months of religious activity in this house could really help shut him up."

"If I had to, Becky should have to," Danny said. "That's only fair. Besides, you were jealous when I had my bar mitzvah. You kept saying how much you wanted one, too, just so you could get gifts."

"Did I?" I asked. I didn't remember much about Danny's bar mitzvah except how depressed I was. He did get a lot of presents, though. And every day in the mail, someone would send him a card filled with money. I never got mail. He never got mail like that again, either, though, and the money all went into the bank, and most of his gifts were boring.

"Mrs. Levinson said there's going to be a bat mitzvah at the temple this Saturday," Mom declared. "Why don't we go, Becky, and you can see for yourself if you want to do it."

"Do I have to?" I asked.

Mom sighed. "I already told you, you don't have to," she said. "And I won't make you. But it was a dream of mine way back when I was pregnant with you. I remember during Lamaze classes Sharon Cohen and I would fantasize about the bar mitzvahs our sons would have. We both knew you girls were going to be boys."

"Your mother also knew Danny was going to be a girl," Dad declared. "He would have been Deborah. Deborah Ruth."

"I'm glad I'm a boy then," Danny said.

"Hold on a second," I said. "You and Sharon talked about my bar mitzvah?"

"And Dina's," Mom replied. "That was when I thought you'd be Richard and Sharon thought Dina would be David. We figured if you were both born within a week of each other, and we all still lived in the same town, then you could have your bar mitzvahs together. We were going to share expenses on the party and really do it up right."

"So if Dina has a bat mitzvah same as me, we could still do it that way," I said. "Study together and read the Torah together and have the party together."

"I think that would be wonderful," Mom said. "And I'm sure Sharon would love it, too."

I sat absolutely still for a moment and tried to remember if Amy Ford had ever said anything about religion. And then it came back to me. She'd said her parents had joined the Methodist church. She wasn't Jewish. No matter how much Dina liked her, they couldn't study for a bat mitzvah together. Not the way Dina and I could. I'd have six months of seeing Dina all alone, no Amy tagging along. Six months, and then we'd have a big party together, to celebrate our bat mitzvahs and the fact that we were best friends again.

I smiled a big, happy, religious smile. "If it's okay with Dina," I said, trying not to crow, "then it's fine with me."

Three

The capital of Vermont is Montpelier. The capital of Virginia is Richmond. The capital of Washington is Olympia." I said that one extra loud. "The capital of West Virginia is Charleston. The capital of Wisconsin is Madison. And the capital of Wyoming is Cheyenne."

"Very good, Becky," Mrs. Maguire said. "And you wrote those lists as I told you to?"

I handed them over to her. They were the neatest lists I'd ever done. I practically curlicued the dots over my "i"s.

Mrs. Maguire checked them out carefully. I stood there waiting for her to dismiss me. She'd kept me after school just like she'd said she would and made sure I really did know my capitals. Which I certainly did. Of course I'd memorized them in strict alphabetical order by state, and I wasn't sure if I could

25

have told her the capital of Tennessee without going through forty-one other capitals first.

"Now, what lessons have you learned from your mistake?" Mrs. Maguire asked me. She put the lists down on her desk, so I figured they must be acceptable.

"Lessons?" I said. "I learned all the state capitals." I wondered if she was going to make me run through them all over again.

"That wasn't a lesson," Mrs. Maguire declared. "That was a class assignment you failed to do properly the first time. I'm talking about lessons that you learned from our talk yesterday."

"Oh, you mean talking about religion is rude," I said. "Stuff like that."

"Yes, Becky," Mrs. Maguire said with a sigh. "Stuff like that."

I looked down at the floor and tried to concentrate. It didn't help that I saw a wad of chewing gum stuck under Billy Fielding's chair. "I learned that talking about religion is rude," I said. "My grandmother thinks so, too."

"You talked to your grandmother about it?" Mrs. Maguire asked.

"I asked my parents," I said. "And they said my grandmother thinks it's rude. Then we talked about religion a lot. Mostly about my uncle Bob. He's gotton real religious lately. But I guess it would be rude to tell you about it."

Mrs. Maguire nodded. "What other lessons did you learn?"

How many did she expect of me? I couldn't be

sure if this was a fill-in-the-blank or an essay question. "I don't know," I finally muttered.

"Did you learn it's always better to come prepared with your assignments done well than to hope you don't get called on in class?" Mrs. Maguire asked.

"Oh, yes," I said. "I certainly learned that lesson."

"And did you learn not to talk back to your teachers?"

I hadn't remembered talking back to Mrs. Maguire, but since I'd prayed that she be struck down dead and painfully, I felt she had every right to feel I had talked back to her. So I nodded. "I'll never talk back to any of my teachers again," I vowed. That still left me free to pray for their slaughter. Dad had taught me to be careful how you define your terms when you negotiate.

"And did you learn that nobody likes a rude little girl?" Mrs. Maguire continued.

I wanted to tell her that I wasn't a little girl, that in six months I'd be regarded as a functioning adult at my temple. That's what a bat mitzvah was all about. Of course I hadn't noticed Danny becoming much more of an adult after his bar mitzvah. But girls mature faster than boys.

"Nobody likes a rude little girl," I repeated. It was probably true, too, even if I wasn't a little girl. I wondered what kind of little girl Mrs. Maguire had been, and whether anybody had ever liked her. I doubted it.

"Very well," Mrs. Maguire said. "You're a smart girl, Becky, and when you do your homework assignments, you do very well in class. I expect

27

quality work from you, and now you know the consequences if you fail to live up to my expectations."

I nodded some more.

"You may now thank me for these valuable lessons and leave," Mrs. Maguire declared.

"Thank you," I said. It took a lot of effort to get the words out. "Good-bye." I grabbed my books and ran out of the room. The minute I was out the door I stuck my tongue out, which was probably a rude-little-girl thing to do, but it felt great anyway.

I was hoping that Dina had stayed in the yard waiting for me the way she had the day before, but she was nowhere I could find her. I stood there for a moment, trying to remember her schedule. It wasn't piano lesson day or gymnastics day. So she was probably home.

I skipped all the way to her house, humming state capitals as I went. I'd gone through all of them once and was back on the capital of North Dakota (Bismarck) when I got to her house.

I rang the bell and Dina opened it right away. "Hi there!" I said. "We have to talk."

"We do?" Dina said, which wasn't the friendliest greeting I could imagine. I ignored her and skipped into her living room. Sitting right there, on the living room sofa, where I always sat, was Amy Ford.

"Oh," I said. "I mean, hi. I mean, what are you doing here?"

"Dina asked me over," Amy said in that soft little voice of hers. She was never a rude little girl. "We were going to work on our science project together."

"I thought you and I were going to do the science project together," I said to Dina. "Remember? We talked about it way back first week of school."

Dina sat down on the sofa next to Amy. "You're always late," she said to me. "I didn't think I could trust you to get your half of the work done on time. So I decided to ask Amy to be my partner."

"But that's not fair!" I said. With Amy and Dina on the sofa, I didn't even know where to sit. "I wouldn't have been late. I'm never late about the important things."

"You were late with your state capitals," Dina replied.

"That's different," I said. "I was reading."

"You're always reading," Dina replied. "And you're always late."

I would have walked out right then, but there was too much at stake. Instead, I sat down on the easy chair that faced the sofa. I felt like I was a million miles away from Dina, while Amy was practically her Siamese twin. "I know my state capitals now," I said. "I just did them for Mrs. Maguire. Do you want to hear?"

"Of course not," Dina said. "I know my capitals. I learned them on time, the same as everybody else in the class. You were the only one who was late, Becky. You're always late."

"I think it's terrible the way Mrs. Maguire kept you after school twice," Amy said. "Mrs. Maguire is not a nice teacher."

"I thought you liked her," I said.

"Oh?" Amy said. "Why?"

I realized it was because I didn't like Amy and I didn't like Mrs. Maguire so I naturally assumed they would like each other. But even if I was a rude mid-sized girl, I knew better than to say that. "I don't know," I said. "That was just what I thought."

"Becky thinks a lot of things without any reason," Dina said.

"I do not," I said. "What are you so mad about anyway, Dina?"

"I am not mad," Dina said. "I just can't trust you to get stuff done on time, that's all. And you always assume we'll do everything together. Sometimes I want to do things with other people and you won't let me. You come right over here without asking my permission or anything. That isn't very polite, Becky."

"I've come right over here my entire life," I said. "And you've come right over to my house, too. You never asked me for permission to come over. You just did."

"Amy asks permission," Dina said.

"My mother makes me," Amy said. "I wish I had a friend I was so close to, I didn't have to ask."

"Dina and I have been best friends forever," I told her. "Since even before we were born."

"Becky!" Dina shouted. "Will you stop that already? You told Amy all about it yesterday."

"That's all right," Amy said. "I think it's very interesting. My parents move around a lot, so there's nobody I've known since before I was born."

"I knew you'd understand," I said to her. "Actually, that's why I came over here today. Without asking permission. There was something I had to talk to Dina about, something that happened before we were born."

"Yeah?" Dina said. "What?"

"It has to do with our bat mitzvahs," I said. "Did you know our mothers used to fantasize about them before we were born? Only they thought we'd be boys, so we'd have bar mitzvahs instead."

"What of it?" Dina asked.

"What exactly is a bat mitzvah?" Amy asked.

"It's a coming-of-age ceremony," I said. "Jews do it. It announces that you're a full member of the community. You read the Torah, that's the Bible in Hebrew, sort of, and you lead the services, and you give a little speech, and then you have a party, and everybody gives you presents. Everyone does it."

"Everyone does not do it," Dina said. "Boys just about have to, but lots of girls don't."

"But more and more are," I said. "And we ought to. Religion isn't just something for boys. It's for girls, too. And in six months we'll be thirteen and we'll be old enough to have bat mitzvahs."

"They sound wonderful," Amy said. "I love going to church."

"It's a lot of work," I said. "But it's worth it. To stand up there in front of the entire congregation and proclaim that you are an adult, just like they are. It's a great moment."

"It doesn't last," Dina declared. "The next day they treat you just like a kid again. Even worse. You have to write all those thank-you notes. I remember when Danny had his bar mitzvah. Your mother was after him to write thank-you notes for weeks after that. Finally she said he couldn't leave the house the whole weekend until he got them done. That doesn't sound like being treated like a grown-up to me."

"If he'd done them right away, it wouldn't have been a problem," I said. I had forgotten about the thank-you notes. That was the problem with having a friend for forever. She remembered all kinds of things that were best forgotten. "Besides, the thank-you notes are worth it for all the good stuff you get. Not to mention the party and the religious part." I tried looking kind of holy when I said it.

"Are you going to have a bat mitzvah?" Amy asked me. It sounded funny when she said it.

I nodded. "That's why I'm here," I declared. "To tell Dina that I'm going to have a bat mitzvah and to tell her to have one, too."

"What makes you think you can tell me anything?" Dina asked.

"To ask you, then," I said. "Does your mother have anything in this house I could eat? I'm famished."

"We were going to have some cookies," Amy said. "Right before you came in."

"Great," I said. I got up and walked to the kitchen. Amy and Dina followed me. I found the cookies and a plate and set them up. I knew that kitchen as well as I knew my own. I only hoped Amy realized it. "Have a cookie, Amy," I said, just in case she needed another demonstration.

"Thank you," she said, taking the one cookie that was missing a little piece. She bit into it delicately. I took a big all-in-one-piece cookie and rammed it into my mouth. "This cookie is delicious," Amy said. "Your mother is a very good baker, Dina."

"Thank you," Dina said.

"Will she bake for your bat mitzvah?" Amy asked.

"Oh, no," I said. "It isn't that kind of party. You have to invite lots of people, all your relatives and friends from school and camp, practically everybody you've ever known. You'd have lots of people to invite, Amy, since you've gone to so many schools, but of course you can't have a bat mitzvah, not being Jewish and all."

Amy nodded and took another little bite. I decided if I had to be stuck on a desert island, she'd be the person to get stuck with. I could out-eat her three to one.

"Dina, do you think you'll have a bat mitzvah?" she asked.

"No," Dina replied.

"But you have to," I said. "That's why I came over. To discuss it with you. Our birthdays are less

33

than a week apart, so we could share the whole thing, the lessons and the service and the party. It would be so much fun."

"You'd be late again," Dina replied. "The way you always are. I'll end up standing there and you'll be late and not know your part and make me look like an idiot. Forget it, Becky."

"I absolutely promise I'll be on time and know everything," I said. "This bat mitzvah is the most important thing in the world to me, Dina. I won't screw it up. I promise, promise, promise."

"But it's so much extra work," Dina said. She'd put down her cookie and was staring at me. That was the first time since I'd gotten there that she actually looked at me, and I figured I was making great progress. "And I have piano lessons and gymnastics."

"I know," I said. "I have clarinet lessons and ballet. We're both busy. But we should never be too busy for God." I personally thought that last sentence was a great touch.

"You stopped ballet last year," Dina declared.

"Oh, that's right," I said. "But I might take it up again. That doesn't matter. What's important is that we both become bat mitzvahs at the same time. Like our mothers dreamed. We owe it to them."

"I don't know," Dina said.

"We owe our mothers everything," Amy said. "My mother dreamed of riding horses in the Olympics, only she had me instead, so now I ride competitively."

"Are you going to be in the Olympics?" I asked.

"Maybe, if I'm good enough," Amy said. "It's been hard, since I keep switching instructors and horses when we move. But I'll keep trying for the sake of my mother."

"You see," I said to Dina. "These things are important."

"What things?" she asked. "Horses?"

"No," I said. "Mothers. And God."

"Mothers and God are very important," Amy said. "Fathers are important, too."

"That's right," I said. "Think how your father must feel. He never had a son to carry on the religious tradition. You have to have a bat mitzvah for your father's sake."

"My father doesn't care," Dina said.

"You'd be surprised," I said. "I didn't think my father would care, either, but you should have heard how he went on about it last night." Of course it was mostly about driving Uncle Bob crazy, but there was no point mentioning that.

"I don't know," Dina said.

"I really think you should," Amy said. "I know it isn't my religion, but it sounds like such a wonderful thing. Would I be able to attend? I'd love to see it."

"I don't think so," I said. "I don't think Christians are allowed to go to bat mitzvahs."

"Of course they can," Dina replied. "You're crazy, Becky."

"How do you know?" I asked.

"Remember when Jennifer Margolis had her bat

mitzvah?" Dina asked. "Last year? Her mother converted to Judaism, so her family was all some kind of Christian, and they were there. Jennifer said they liked it even more than the Margolises."

"All right, then," I said. "You can come, Amy. And you can certainly come to the party."

"That's wonderful," Amy said. "I'm so excited for you."

"I haven't said I'm going to do it yet," Dina declared. "Give me some time to think about it."

"Sure," I said, but inside I was singing. Sometimes I knew Dina better than she knew herself, and when she said she had to think, that meant she had already decided but just didn't know it. That's what happens when you have a best friend for longer than your entire life. You know them even better than they know themselves, even better sometimes, than you know yourself. If Dina said she had to think, then that meant I could count on six months of being alone with her and God.

Four

"Come in, come in," Mom said to Sharon, Ted, and Dina as she opened the front door a couple of nights later. "Let me take your jackets. There's cake and coffee waiting."

"This is so exciting," Sharon replied. "Come on Ted, Dina, let's show some enthusiasm here."

"Becky's enthusiastic enough for all of us," Mom declared. Dina and her parents followed Mom into the living room, where Dad, Danny, and I were waiting for them. Having the two families get together was Mom's idea. I hardly had to suggest it to her at all.

"You take cream in your coffee, right, Ted?" Mom asked, as she began pouring and serving. Ted nodded.

"These cakes look delicious," Sharon remarked. She bit into one. "They are delicious. Where did you get them?"

"That new bakery on South Main," Mom replied.

"I've been meaning to try it," Sharon said. "Now I know I'll have to."

"They bake wonderful breads there, too," Mom said. "I've taken to going there a couple of times a week. And they couldn't be nicer."

"Bakery talk," Ted said. "Come on, ladies, we're here to discuss business."

"May I be excused?" Danny asked. He'd stayed long enough to take a couple of the cakes and wrap them in a napkin. "I'm in the middle of a really good book."

"Please stay, Danny," Mom said. "We might need your expertise. You became a bar mitzvah a lot more recently than any of the rest of us."

"My bar mitzvah was a nightmare," Ted said conversationally. "It was right before my parents' divorce, and they were barely speaking to each other. Dad moved out a week later. I could never figure out if they stayed together for the sake of the bar mitzvah, or whether the bar mitzvah was what finally drove them apart."

"Your parents are crazy," Sharon declared. "It's a wonder you turned out as well as you did."

"My point is that bar mitzvahs can cause a lot of stress," Ted said. "Mine certainly did. My parents were screaming, my grandparents were screaming, one of my aunts had to be carted away, she got so hysterical. Worse than a funeral. Almost as bad as our wedding. Is that really something we want to put our daughters through?"

"I liked my bar mitzvah," Dad declared. "I liked

the feeling of working toward a goal and then achieving it. I remember enjoying the same sensation vicariously when Danny was preparing. It's a rite of passage, and I think it's great that it's available for our daughters nowadays."

"Have a cake, Dina," I said. She was sitting quietly in a chair, not quite looking at any of us. I knew I pretty much had her convinced, but I wanted to make sure everything was set before I started lessons. The worst thing I could imagine would be to agree to the bat mitzvah, get halfway through the lessons, and then have Dina change her mind. The one way I knew I could keep her going was by convincing her parents to go halvsies with mine on everything. Which was why I casually suggested to Mom we get both families together. And Mom, still remembering her Lamaze fantasies, agreed instantly.

"Having a bar mitzvah was okay," Danny declared. "The work was hard, but I liked standing up there and reading the Torah. The party was great. Can I go now?"

Dad laughed. "Go," he said. "But be on call. We might need you to answer a question or two."

"I'll be in my room," Danny replied. He gathered up another couple of cakes and went upstairs. We watched as he left and listened to him walk to his bedroom. The silence felt funny.

"Dina tells us this bat mitzvah was all your idea, Becky," Ted said. "I'm surprised. I didn't think you went to temple very often."

It hadn't occurred to me that either of Dina's

parents would resist the idea of the joint bat mitzvahs. They both loved me, the way my parents loved Dina, like unofficial nieces. And religion was one of those things grown-ups were supposed to approve of automatically, along with good grades and saving your money.

"I haven't been going often enough," I admitted. "And at first I wasn't so excited about the idea. But then I gave it some thought and I realized how important it could be."

"In what way?" Ted asked. Ted's a reporter, and that's almost as bad as being a lawyer when it comes to asking questions.

I didn't know just how to answer that. The most important way was it gave me something to do with Dina that Amy couldn't do with us, but that was just the kind of answer that would get all this bat mitzvah business thrown out immediately.

"It's important to God," I said. I hoped Ted wouldn't ask me how, since I certainly didn't know. But religion was all about God, and bat mitzvahs were all about religion, so I figured if I used God as an excuse no one could question me. Right then I wouldn't have minded a little bit of Mrs. Maguire's attitude about discussing religion.

"God," Ted said. "Well, it's hard to argue with God."

"I've picked a few fights in my day," Dad declared. "But God always ends up the winner."

"Don't make jokes," Mom said. "We're talking about our faith here, the faith of our parents and grandparents, and great-great-great-great-grandparents. We're talking about a heritage we want to pass down to our children, so they can pass it down to theirs. Bar mitzvahs aren't just about God, or turning thirteen. They're about being part of something bigger than we are, something millions of people have died to maintain. I'm proud of being Jewish, and I'm proud that my daughter wants to declare her commitment to that faith."

Sharon applauded. I felt terrible. It had never occurred to me that that was what I was doing. I just thought I was making sure Dina and I would stay friends forever.

"I still don't know," Ted said. "That was a lovely speech, Annie, and it isn't that I disagree with any of it. But a bat mitzvah takes a lot of time, and Dina is very busy with her piano and gymnastics. Not to mention schoolwork and helping around the house. I don't want her to feel she has to give one activity up just to prepare for a bat mitzvah. I don't think that would be fair to her."

"Dina, do you think you have the time for everything?" Mom asked. I was glad she was the one asking. It was going to be hard for Dina to say she didn't, after Mom's speech about all those generations.

"I can manage, I guess," Dina replied.

I breathed a sigh of relief. Dina hadn't sounded too thrilled, but that would come with time. I knew Dina. Once she got involved with something, it was the only thing that really mattered to her. The trick was getting her to start it in the first place.

"Such enthusiasm," Ted said. I guess he didn't understand Dina as well as I did.

"There's something I'd like to say," Sharon declared. "Ted, you remember your bar mitzvah as being unpleasant, full of family problems. I'm sorry it wasn't a happy event for you, but that had nothing to do with Judaism. Anything going on in your family right then would have been difficult and unpleasant. But it's important to me that Dina became a bat mitzvah in a way that Annie didn't discuss."

"What's that?" Mom asked. I loved the way the mothers were cooperating. If it were up to them, Dina and I would be best friends at least through our double wedding.

Sharon put her coffee cup down. "I was very religious when I was about eleven," she said. "Not because my family was. I just developed that way. And it drove me crazy that I couldn't do anything about it. So I insisted on having a bat mitzvah. The synagogue I went to wasn't real big on them; as a matter of fact, I was only the second or third girl ever to have one. And they did a real little throw-away service for me. It was Friday night rather than Saturday morning, and of course I wasn't allowed anywhere near the Torah. I read a little bit from the Bible and said a prayer or two, and then everyone congratulated me as if that were enough. Only it wasn't enough for me. I felt cheated. It was as if they were saying Jewish women weren't as important as Jewish men, which of course was exactly what they were saying. Only they wouldn't admit it at the time. Instead they said Jewish women were different from men and should be satisfied with their role."

"I know exactly what you're talking about," Mom declared. "That's one reason why I insisted we join a Reform temple, one where men and women were treated equally."

"And it's why I want Dina to have a bat mitzvah equal to the bar mitzvah Danny had," Sharon said. "I want my daughter to know she's the equal of any man in the eyes of God and her religious community."

"After that speech, how can we say no?" Dad said. "It's like telling Becky and Dina that they can't be President of the United States because they're girls."

"Running for President doesn't cost as much as a bat mitzvah party," Ted said. "I hate sounding like the devil's advocate, but Sharon and I have been to a few of those parties, and they're getting awfully elaborate. We were at one last year with a five-piece band and dancing until two in the morning, and a fountain that spewed champagne. None of which had anything to do with being equal in the eyes of God or making a commitment to the faith of our parents."

"We don't have to do anything like that," Dad declared.

"Wait a second," I said. "I want a party."

Everyone laughed. "The truth comes out," Ted said.

I turned bright red. "Danny had a party," I said. "If Dina and I are his equals, shouldn't we have one, too?"

"She's got you there, Ted," Sharon declared.

"She's a lawyer's daughter," Dad said. "We're not saying no party, Becky. We're saying no champagne fountains. You may recall Danny got along just fine without one of those."

"I want a party, too," Dina said. "Something I can invite all my friends to."

She meant Amy, but since there was no way I was going to keep her out of the party, I didn't even try. Besides, in six months time, Amy would be just another friend, and not someone Dina did her science projects with.

"If we share party expenses, we should be able to manage something just a little bit fancy," Mom said. "Nothing tasteless or extravagant. But a lot of our guest lists would overlap anyway, especially with the girls' classmates. No champagne fountains, but an ice sculpture or two."

"Lots of pretty flowers," Sharon said. "The bat mitzvahs will be in the spring, right around the girls' birthdays. We should be able to get beautiful flower arrangements."

"I'll have to invite my mother and my father," Ted said. "You know what that's like."

"We'll put your mother in with Hal's relatives, and your father in with Annie's," Sharon replied. "They won't even realize the other one is there."

44

"Does this mean we're really having it?" I asked. "The bat mitzvahs and the party and everything?"

"I guess so," Ted said. "Just as long as you realize the everything includes lessons and studying and going to temple and stage fright."

"It sounds wonderful," I said. "Doesn't it, Dina?"

"Sure," Dina said. "Especially the stage fright."

"Don't scare the girls," Sharon said. "Danny survived, after all. And you girls are as smart as he is."

"I heard that!" Danny called from his bedroom.

We all laughed, even Dina. Then we started talking about bat mitzvahs and parties and school and jobs and it felt like a normal evening again. Even Danny came back down and told us about parties he'd gone to. Dina relaxed and acted the way she always did. I could tell my plan was going to work perfectly.

The Cohens left around nine. Mom and Danny picked up the plates and coffee cups and Dad walked over to the phone.

"Who are you calling?" Mom asked him.

"I haven't decided," Dad replied. "Should you call Bob, or should I? He's your brother, but he might take the news better from a man."

"What news?" Mom asked.

"About Becky's bat mitzvah," Dad said. "About her commitment to the faith and her equality in the eyes of God. It should drive him crazy."

"I love it when you're fervent," Mom said. "But neither one of us can call him right now."

"Why not?" Dad asked.

45

"It's Friday night," Mom replied. "And Bob is no longer answering the phone on the Sabbath. You're going to have to wait until after sundown tomorrow."

"Drat," Dad said. "Next time we decide to commit to the faith of our forebears, let's do it on a weekday night."

"You can do it any time you want," Mom said, giving me a kiss on the cheek. "I'm so proud of you, honey. I know this bat mitzvah is going to be something you'll look back on all the rest of your life with pride and satisfaction."

I was already looking at it that way, but I just smiled.

"My parents," Dad said. "They answer the phones Friday night. Can you imagine their reaction?"

"They'll be thrilled," Mom said. "You'd better call them fast, though, before they go to bed."

So Dad dialed their number. Only instead of saying hi, he was silent, which meant he got their answering machine. "This is Hal," he said. "Your son. I'm calling with great news about Becky. Call us when you have a chance." He hung up and looked disgruntled. "When a son has to speak to his parents' answering machine, what is this world coming to?" he asked.

"That's right, it's Friday," Mom said. "All your parents' favorite shows are on Friday night. They turn on their machine so they won't be bothered."

Dad sighed. "Here I have this great news and no one to share it with," he said.

46

"It's enough we know it now," Mom said. "The rest of the world can wait to find out."

That was exactly how I felt, too. I knew the news, and so did Dina, and so did Amy. Everyone else could wait.

Five

Hello, girls. I'm Rabbi Greenberg."

I wondered if Dina was as startled as I was. Rabbi Greenberg was a woman. Not that I minded having the rabbi who was going to tutor us for our bat mitzvahs be a woman. I was just surprised.

"I'm Dina Cohen," Dina said, so I guess she was able to make her mouth move faster than I could. "And this is Becky Weiss."

"Hi, Dina, Becky," Rabbi Greenberg said. She smiled at both of us and I could see she was young, as grown-ups went, and kind of pretty. She was wearing a wedding ring. I wondered if her husband was a rabbi, too, and if they argued over who got to say which blessings. My mother always said it was better to marry someone in a different field.

"Why don't you sit down," Rabbi Greenberg

said, and so Dina and I did. We were in the rabbi's study, and it was lined with books and certificates. But there were also some photographs of kids.

"I took them in Israel," Rabbi Greenberg said. "My husband and I went there on our honeymoon."

"Is he a rabbi, too?" Dina asked. I was relieved that she had. I had the feeling Mrs. Maguire would have regarded it as a rude question, so I didn't think I should.

Rabbi Greenberg smiled. "He's an oral surgeon," she replied.

"That's good," I said. "I mean, my mother would think so."

"So did my mother," Rabbi Greenberg declared, but she laughed, and then we all did. "All right, Dina, Becky, shall we get started?"

"Sure," Dina said. "We're here to study for our bat mitzvahs."

"That's right," Rabbi Greenberg said. "We'll study reading the Torah and leading the service. But I want our time together to be about more than the one day of your bat mitzvahs. I want us to think about Judaism as well, and what it means to become a bat mitzvah."

I nodded, although I didn't really know what she was talking about.

"Did you know that Judaism is the oldest religion currently being practiced on earth?" Rabbi Greenberg asked. "Its only competition is Hinduism, and that's evolved more diversely. The rules of Judaism, the prayers, date back three, even four thousand years. Think of that. When you become a bat mitzvah, you'll be joining a line of men and women that is four thousand years old."

"That's what my mother said," I declared. "Not quite that way, but that's what she meant. She said it was the religion of our great-great-great-grandparents."

"And then some," Rabbi Greenberg declared. "Now of course Judaism has changed throughout the centuries. It's a living faith, not a museum piece. For example, bar mitzvahs. They're a relatively recent custom. They began in the Middle Ages."

"But that was a long time ago," Dina said. "What about bat mitzvahs?"

"They're even more recent," Rabbi Greenberg said. "They're pretty much a twentieth-century American invention."

"My mother had a bat mitzvah," Dina said. "And she said she was practically the first one in her synagogue to have one."

"Even when I became a bat mitzvah, it wasn't common," Rabbi Greenberg replied. "But now, especially in Reform temples, there's a feeling that girls should be treated exactly as boys, and have the same opportunity to be accepted into the community. Because one of the important things about Judaism is that it is a community. There are Jews all over the world, in Africa and Asia, as well as Europe and Israel and right here. But we are all one people. When you become a bat mitzvah, you will join in the Jewish community with Ethiopians and Chinese and Russians, as well as the community represented in our temple. And all those Jews, no matter where they're from, represent part of the unbroken line that dates back four thousand years."

"Wow," Dina said. "It's like a giant family."

"That's exactly what it's like," Rabbi Greenberg said. "And like any family, it has its family quarrels and its family tragedies and its family joys. Do you think you know any of those, the quarrels or the tragedies or the joys?"

"I know a quarrel," I said. "My father and my uncle Bob."

"That's not what Rabbi Greenberg means," Dina said.

"It sounds interesting anyway," Rabbi Greenberg said. "Go on, Becky."

"Well, my father isn't very observant," I said. "Actually, he hardly goes to temple at all. And my uncle Bob, lately he's been dating this woman who's really religious and now he goes to synagogue and he observes the Sabbath completely, and he won't even eat at our house because we don't keep kosher. So that's a family quarrel because we're all Jewish, right?"

Rabbi Greenberg nodded. "It certainly is," she said. "There are lots of different ways of practicing Judaism. And naturally the people who observe it one way think that theirs is the right way, so they quarrel with other Jews."

"See?" I said to Dina.

"Well, I thought the rabbi meant something big," she said. "Like the Holocaust."

"The Holocaust certainly was a tragedy," Rabbi

Greenberg said. "Not just for the Jews, but for all humanity. What do you know about it, Dina?"

"I know that Adolph Hitler was the dictator of Germany," Dina replied. "And he hated Jews, so he set up death camps to kill them. And six million Jews died there. My grandmother's aunts and uncles and cousins were killed, but my grandfather's family had moved to the United States way before then, so they were all okay."

"Lots of people have hated the Jews throughout the centuries," Rabbi Greenberg said. "Jews have been persecuted for their faith, and yet we've never given it up. Even today, there are countries where it's dangerous to be a Jew."

"Like the Soviet Union?" I said. "Jews want to leave there, but the government doesn't let them all go."

"The Soviet Union was the country I was thinking of, too," Rabbi Greenberg said. "As a matter of fact, one of the new traditions of bar and bat mitzvahs involves Soviet Jews. Do you want to hear about it?"

"Sure," Dina said.

"Do we get to invite some?" I asked.

"Don't be dumb," Dina said.

"In a way, Becky is right," Rabbi Greenberg said. I liked Rabbi Greenberg more and more. "In the Soviet Union, it's a danger to practice any religion, including Judaism. But religion dies hard. People want to believe, and they're willing to risk death to be a part of their faith. We, in America, do what we can to help, and one thing we do is to share our celebrations. We pair off, or "twin," bar mitzvahs and bat mitzvahs with Soviet Jewish children who cannot have their own. Would you like to be twinned with two Russian girls?"

"Sure," Dina said.

"Would they come?" I asked. I was still worried about guest lists.

"Only in spirit," Rabbi Greenberg replied. "Let me check the list here." She opened her desk drawer and found the sheet of paper she needed. "There are two girls here who should become bat mitzvahs the same time you girls will," she said. "One is named Olga Abromowitz, and she lives in Moscow. The other is named Olga Levine, and she lives in Leningrad."

"They're both named Olga," I said. "Won't that get confusing?"

"Maybe," Rabbi Greenberg said. "But I think we can all handle it."

"How does this twinning business work?" I asked.

"However you want it to," Rabbi Greenberg replied. "Some people put the names of the Russian children on their invitations to indicate the ceremony is being shared. And you can have a chair set up in the temple with the person's name on it. There are a lot of different ways of doing it. We can discuss them in greater detail later if you and your parents decide to do it."

"Are there any other different things we should

know about?" I asked. I wanted to get them all out of the way, so if there was any more convincing that had to be done, I'd know what to expect.

"There is another new tradition that I'm very fond of," Rabbi Greenberg replied. "As you know, there are many hungry and needy people living right here in this area."

"Do we have to invite them, too?" Dina asked. I was glad I wasn't the only one worried about guest lists.

"We don't invite them, but we do share with them," Rabbi Greenberg said. "What you can do, and it would go on your invitations, is request that your guests bring canned goods to the bat mitzvah party. The foods are gathered, and then the next day they're donated to the local soup kitchens and shelters."

"I like that," I said. "It's like everybody gets presents, not just the two of us."

"That's exactly what it's like," Rabbi Greenberg said. "And if your parents decide to do it, have them call me, and I'll help with the arrangements."

"I think we got sidetracked," Dina said. "We were discussing tragedies and joy."

"That's right," Rabbi Greenberg said. "Other than the occasion of your bat mitzvahs, can you think of another joy belonging to the Jewish family?"

"Israel?" I asked.

"Israel," Rabbi Greenberg said. "Do you know when Israel became a country, Becky?"

"We'll be reading it in Hebrew," I said. "No one will understand. What will you die from?"

"It says not to lie down with beasts," Dina said. "This whole chapter is about nakedness and beasts."

"Maybe it sounds better in Hebrew," I said.

"You do chapter eighteen," Dina said. "I'll take chapter nineteen."

"You don't even know what's in it," I said.

"It's got to be improvement," Dina declared. "If I have to read about nakedness and beasts even in Hebrew, I'll start laughing, and then I'll just die."

"Let's check out nineteen," I said.

"Nineteen looks pretty good," Dina said, skimming it. "It mostly sounds like the ten commandments. Oh, this part is nice."

"What?" I asked. Dina was hogging the Bible, but I had a feeling it was a sin to grab it from her.

"It says here not to harvest all the grapes, but to leave some for the poor and the stranger," she said.

"If we have people bring food to our party, it'll be like that," I said. I would have liked to have read that part, but I had a feeling if I pushed Dina into nakedness and beasts, she'd forget the whole business. "What else is there?"

"It says you shouldn't be a talebearer," Dina said. "That's great. Who would have thought God cared about tattletales?"

"God cares about everything," I replied. "That's why He's God."

"He certainly seems to care about nakedness," Dina said. "Oh, I don't believe this."

"What?" I asked. "More beasts?"

57

"No," Dina said. "It says 'thou shalt love thy neighbor as thyself.' That's famous."

I tried not to scowl. Dina got all the stuff about sharing food and not telling tales and loving thy neighbor and I got don't uncover Uncle Bob's nakedness.

"You don't mind if we divide it up that way?" Dina asked me. "The rest of this chapter looks pretty boring, although there is some stuff about not hanging out with wizards."

"It's okay," I said with a sigh. "But I get to pick which Russian girl I want first."

"They're both named Olga," Dina replied.

"I know," I said. "But I want the one in Leningrad. She sounds more exotic."

"She's all yours," Dina said. "Just as long as I don't have to read about lying with beasts."

"It's a deal," I said. We even shook hands on it. Dina took hers away, though, when her phone rang.

"Oh, hi, Amy," she said, and my stomach instantly clenched. "I can't really talk now. No, Becky is here, and we're reading the Bible together. That's right, for our bat mitzvahs. It's really interesting." She was silent for a moment. "Maybe you'd better get a different partner for the science project," she said. "I'm going to be really busy studying for my bat mitzvah. It might make more sense if Becky and I did something together, since we're going to be seeing so much of each other anyway."

And in that moment, I added another thing to the list of joys that my faith had brought me.

Six

I owe you a thank you," Dina said to me a few weeks later as we were walking to our bat mitzvah lesson.

"What for?" I asked her.

"For coming up with this whole idea," she replied. "The bat mitzvah. I never would have decided to do it on my own, and I'm so glad now. I love everything about it."

"Even the extra work?" I asked. We had to practice reading our Torah and Haftorah portions over and over again, and Rabbi Greenberg gave us extra assignments as well, books to read so we could talk about the history of Jews and the meaning of our bat mitzvah portions. Not that we'd gone into too much detail about uncovering nakedness. I guess Rabbi Greenberg figured we could work that out for ourselves.

"I love the work," Dina said. "I love really

studying the Bible. I've been reading it to myself at night before I go to bed. In English, because that's so much easier, but it's the same Bible after all. And I pray every night now before I go to sleep. I say the Sh'ma. I whisper it, so Mom and Dad won't hear, but God will."

"That's great," I said. "I bet God is real pleased."

"And I'm trying to figure out how to get my parents to keep kosher," Dina continued. "At least in our house. I told Mom I was going to, and she was just going to have to accept the fact that I wouldn't eat bacon anymore, or shrimp, or lots of other things she cooks really well, and she shrugged her shoulders and said 'this too shall pass,' only it won't. I love being Jewish, even if it does mean no bacon."

"You sound like my uncle Bob," I said and stomped through a pile of dried leaves. They made a nice crackly noise.

"I wish I could be more like him," Dina declared. "And really observe the Sabbath. But it's hard not to turn on lights and stuff when everyone else in the house does. You forget. And all my favorite TV shows are on Friday night."

"Now you sound just like my grandparents," I said.

"I'm going to be a rabbi when I grow up," Dina said. "You're the first person I've told. I'm going to be a rabbi and pray and study all the time. I'm going to devote my life to my faith. What do you think?"

"I think that's wonderful," I replied. Actually, I thought it was pretty silly. Last year, when Dina had her appendix out, she was going to be a doctor and devote her life to healing. And the year before that, when her grandmother was mugged, she was going to be a police officer and devote her life to bringing criminals to justice. Unless Dina had as many lives as a cat, she was going to have to devote her life to changing her careers.

"So, thank you," Dina said. "Because if it hadn't been for you, I never would have realized what it was I wanted to do. And I love everything about it. I even love that stupid canned goods idea. I thought at first it would be embarrassing to have it on our invitations, but now that we've been studying Leviticus, I can see how canned goods are just like grapes of the vineyard. Maybe when I'm a rabbi, I'll open a shelter for the homeless. I could call it the Leviticus House. What do you think?"

"Maybe there won't be homeless by then," I said.

"That would be nice," Dina said. "I guess I could open a school instead and call it the Leviticus House."

"Good idea," I said.

Dina was full of good ideas and she told me all of them until we settled down with Rabbi Greenberg for our lesson. I was happy for her, even if I wondered what her next lifelong devotion was going to be. The bat mitzvah plan had worked perfectly. Dina hardly saw anything of Amy anymore. Instead, we were always together, just the way we used to be. Sometimes we studied our regular schoolwork, and sometimes we worked on our bat mitzvahs, and sometimes we planned for the party. There was always something to do, something to talk about. And now that Dina had decided to be a rabbi and was grateful to me, there'd be even more to talk about and share. We were best friends since forever again, at least for the time being.

Dina had lots of things to contribute that day during our lesson, but I didn't feel like talking. At least not while Dina was there. When our lesson finally ended, though, I asked Rabbi Greenberg if I could stay a few extra minutes to ask her some things.

"Certainly," she said, smiling at me. I really liked Rabbi Greenberg. Some kids I'd talked to were scared of the rabbis who gave them bar mitzvah lessons, so I knew how lucky I was.

"I'm going home, then," Dina said. "I'll talk to you tonight, Becky."

"Sure," I said. A month ago I would have been thrilled to hear her say that. Now I took it for granted. I watched as she left the room, and then I turned to face the rabbi.

"What kind of questions do you have, Becky?" she asked me.

"I don't know," I said. "Big ones."

"All right," she said. "Where do you want to begin?"

"There's a lot I don't understand," I told her. "Not about our studies. I'm enjoying them, and I can understand them pretty well."

"I know you can," Rabbi Greenberg said. "You and Dina are delights to teach. You're both very bright girls and it's obvious how important becoming bat mitzvahs is to you."

I cleared my throat and looked at the pictures of Israel. Rabbi Greenberg touched me gently on my arm. "But that doesn't answer your questions," she said. "Do you want to start asking them?"

I nodded. "What I don't understand is God," I said. "And the Jews."

"In what way?" Rabbi Greenberg asked.

"Well, if God likes the Jews so much, how come we've had to suffer?" I asked. "Why didn't God kill Hitler, or have him never be born, or if he had to be born, why couldn't he have been someone different and not been dictator, and all those Jews would have lived. And it wasn't just Hitler. Jews get killed all the time."

"Not only Jews get killed," Rabbi Greenberg said. "A lot of people have suffered throughout history because of who they are or where they were born."

"Well, I don't understand any of that, either," I said. "Doesn't God care?"

"What do you think?" Rabbi Greenberg asked me.

"I don't know," I said. "That's why I'm asking you. You're the rabbi. Don't they teach you the answers in rabbinical school?"

"They teach some possible answers," she replied. "But only God knows the real meaning."

"Well, what are the answers they teach you?" I

63

asked. "I could use some answers. All this is bothering me."

"I can see that," she said. "And you're right to be bothered. Many, many people have asked the same questions, and of course there is no right answer."

"Are you telling me there isn't any answer?" I said.

"No," Rabbi Greenberg said. "Faith is an answer. Believing that just because it isn't for people to understand, doesn't mean God's reasons are invalid, is an answer. If you trust in God, then you trust in what He does, even if it hurts you. That's how most people answer your questions."

"Faith," I said, trying it out. "What are other answers?"

Rabbi Greenberg smiled. "I knew I was going to like you from the moment you told me about your uncle Bob," she declared. "All right. Other answers. Some people might say that something good comes from all the pain. For example, there might not have been a state of Israel if it hadn't been for Adolph Hitler and the Holocaust. Just like a lot of people died in the Civil War so that the slaves would be set free. Out of pain and suffering something good emerges."

"I don't see why the good can't just emerge without the pain and suffering," I told her. "God could have just had it so there weren't any slaves. He must not have liked slavery. He set us free in Egypt, after all."

"Then how's this for an explanation," Rabbi Greenberg said. "Perhaps things have to get really awful so that human goodness can shine through. Think of the Righteous Gentiles, the people who defied the Nazis by helping to keep Jews alive, even though their own lives were at risk as a result. Or the people who ran the Underground Railroad and helped slaves escape to Canada. Maybe things have to be very, very dark sometimes so that the beacon of light can shine brighter."

"But if God's in charge, then why aren't things light all the time?" I asked. "Why are there homeless people and wars and AIDS?"

"Do you want to know what I think?" Rabbi Greenberg asked. "Just my opinion. You don't have to believe it."

"Sure," I said. "You're a very smart person. I'd like to know what you think."

"I think God deliberately created us imperfect," Rabbi Greenberg declared. "So that we can strive toward something, toward becoming better human beings. A lot of times we fail because we don't pay attention to the rules He set forth for us. But we have to keep trying. God cares about the effort we make. He watches us try. And He roots for us to succeed."

"Oh," I said. "Does that mean Jews are bad, too? Imperfect?"

"I certainly am," Rabbi Greenberg said. "Are you perfect, Becky?"

I shook my head. "I don't think I ever will be,

either," I said. "So I guess I'll just keep on disappointing God."

"I didn't mean it that way," Rabbi Greenberg said. "Oh, dear. That wasn't what I meant at all. You won't disappoint God unless you do something really dreadful. I'm sure Adolph Hitler was a big disappointment to God. But God expects the rest of us to fail on occasion and not be as good as we could be, and not follow His commandments all the time. The idea is to try, and to know that we please God by trying. And we please ourselves. I know I always feel better if I do something good than if I do something not so good. Don't you?"

I thought about it. "A few weeks ago, I didn't know my state capitals and my teacher found out and she called on me and I made an idiot of myself," I said. "So my teacher made me learn them all and the next day she kept me after school and I recited them and I got them all right. I felt really bad not knowing the capitals when she called on me and I guess I felt better when I knew them."

"You guess?" Rabbi Greenberg said.

I shrugged my shoulders. "I was so mad I had to learn them that it didn't feel that much better when I did," I replied. "But it was better than making an idiot of myself. At least it was less embarrassing."

"How about this bat mitzvah?" Rabbi Greenberg asked. "It's something good that you're doing. Don't you feel good about yourself knowing you're sharing it with your best friend and your family and your other friends and the members of the temple and even a girl in Russia you may never meet?"

"Dina's really excited about it," I said. "And so's my mother and I guess my Olga in Russia is, too."

"And you're not?" Rabbi Greenberg asked.

"I don't know," I said. "I just wish I understood things better."

"I wish you did, too," Rabbi Greenberg said. "But I'm glad you're asking the questions. Most kids don't bother. Most adults, for that matter. They just figure if that's what the rabbi says, then that must be the truth. But the ones who ask the questions, they're the ones who really care. And that's so important, Becky."

"Thank you," I said. Frankly, I wished she had better answers for me. When I was little and had a question, I'd ask Danny and he'd always come up with an answer for me. Sometimes it wasn't the right one, but it always sounded good. Maybe I should ask Rabbi Greenberg to talk to Danny about why God behaved the way He did. They could figure out a whole bunch of answers to tell me.

I thanked the rabbi some more, though, and left her office. As I started walking home, I heard someone call my name. I turned around, and there was Amy Ford.

"What are you doing here?" I asked.

"I was waiting for you," she said. "I knew you and Dina had your lesson today, and I wanted to talk to you."

"About what?" I asked, starting my walk home. I didn't know which direction Amy lived in, but if she wanted to walk where I was going, there was nothing I could do to stop her.

"About Dina," she said, in that quiet voice of hers. One thing about Amy. You had to give her all your attention to make sure you knew what she was saying. "Has Dina stopped liking me?"

"I don't know," I said. "Ask Dina."

"I can't," Amy declared. "If I ask Dina, and she has stopped liking me, then she'll be all embarrassed and she'll have to lie. And if she does still like me, but she stopped being my friend for some other reason, then she'll be all embarrassed and she'll have to lie."

"You've been giving this a lot of thought, haven't you?" I said.

"Dina was the first friend I made here," Amy said. "I've made other friends since then, but Dina was the first kid who came up to me and was nice. It gets hard sometimes when you move around a lot and have to make new friends almost every year. It's easier if they're nice to you at the beginning. And I like Dina. She's nice and she's funny. I liked you, too, but you didn't like me, so there was no point trying to be your friend."

"So if we're not friends, why are you asking me about Dina?" I said, feeling very uncomfortable.

"Because you know Dina better than anybody," Amy declared. "I thought maybe she had talked to you about me and you could tell me why she doesn't like me anymore. If she doesn't. Or why she doesn't want to be friends with me anymore if she does like me still."

I wished very hard that Amy would go away. I had enough on my mind without her. "I really think you should ask Dina," I said. "Even if she will just lie."

"I'm asking you," Amy replied, and even in her soft voice, I could hear her words loud and clear. "What's going on with Dina, Becky?"

"She's just busy, that's all," I said. "It isn't easy studying to become a bat mitzvah, you know. Or maybe you don't know, being a Methodist and all, but it's a lot of work. And Dina's really enjoying it. Just today she told me she wants to be a rabbi when she grows up. Maybe you could become a minister and then the two of you could do lots of stuff together. I think they have interfaith breakfasts once a month."

"You really don't like me, do you, Becky," Amy said. "Why not?"

Because you're there, is what I wanted to answer. Because my best friend liked you more than she liked me, if only for a little while. Because you have good manners and you talk quietly and you take the cookie that's a little bit broken. I don't like you for lots of reasons, Amy Ford, I thought, but I didn't say any of that.

"Does it matter why I don't like you?" I said instead. "I thought you cared why Dina doesn't like you."

"I don't care about either of you!" Amy said as loudly as I'd ever heard her say anything. "Goodbye, Becky. I'm sorry if I bothered you."

"I'm sorry, too," I whispered, but she didn't hear

me. I stood there watching her run away, watching the birds fly in their formations, watching the leaves fall, and I thought about how I was supposed to love my neighbor as myself, and how Jews could be bad people, too, and how the important thing to God was that we tried, and I felt awful.

all of them this time, and left the silent house. The day was beautiful, one of those perfect November days when the sun is still bright enough to take the chill out of the air, but everything feels crisp and clean and full of promise. It was the kind of day that made you feel like you could conquer the universe.

I had all my books, and I started walking real fast to school. I wasn't so late that I had to run, but there was no time for dawdling, either. The trees had all lost their leaves, but there were still some mums around, and a fair amount of birds. I looked up at one that was perched on a telephone pole, and then I stared up at the sky, which was absolutely blue, and that was when the awful thing happened.

I looked up at that sky and realized there wasn't any God.

That was it. It wasn't like someone wrote a telegram and put it up there for me to see. There was no thunder or lightning, nothing dramatic. I just looked up at the sky and knew there wasn't any God.

It all seemed so sensible. All those things I didn't understand, all those questions that didn't have answers, all the pain and suffering and even the good things happened, because they just happened. There wasn't any God. We were on our own.

I knew I wasn't the only person who had decided there was no God, but I didn't know just who else felt the way I did so that I could ask them how it happened to them. And frankly, I didn't have that much time to analyze it for myself. I was late for school. God or no God, I had to start moving.

I think if I hadn't been late, I would have realized right away what an awful thing it was to decide there was no God. But my mind was on other things, and it stayed on other things as I ran to make up the lost time, rushed up the school steps as the final bell was ringing, sat down in class, and was greeted by a surprise quiz in English. That's a terrible way to start a week, nearly being late and then a surprise quiz. You don't have much time to think about theology when things are going like that.

The rest of the morning was better, but it was busy, too. And since it didn't bother me that there wasn't any God, I didn't think much about it even when I had the chance. The couple of moments I did have, I found I liked the idea. It made so much sense to me that I felt better having it all figured out. I knew there was a lot I should be thinking about, but it would just have to wait. We played soccer in gym. I thought about that instead.

So it wasn't until lunch that I realized the awful part. Dina found me, and we carried our trays together to the end of a table. The cafeteria was always noisy. I wondered how Amy managed to make herself heard when she ate there. I looked around for her then and found her sitting with a couple of other girls. She wasn't alone. I had nothing to feel bad about, I decided.

Dina and I started by talking about the surprise

English quiz. "On a Monday morning," Dina groaned. "That's the meanest thing I've ever heard of."

"I'm sure you did okay," I told her. "You're always prepared."

"I may be prepared but my brain isn't awake yet," Dina replied. "No one's is first thing Monday morning."

"I know," I said. "I left my math book at home and had to run back to get it."

"I was wondering where you were," Dina said. "I got to the schoolyard a few minutes early. I thought we might talk about the bat mitzvahs some more."

"What about them?" I asked.

Dina covered her face, but then she giggled. "I've forgotten my Olga's name again," she admitted. "I'll die if I have to ask Rabbi Greenberg one more time what my Olga's last name is. She's already had to tell me three times."

"It's Abromowitz," I said. "Mine is Levine."

"Abromowitz," Dina said. "You definitely got the better Olga."

"You got the better Torah portion," I replied. "Besides, we don't know anything about our Olgas. Maybe yours is really brave and noble. Mine could just be boring."

"She might be boring but at least I could remember her name," Dina declared. "Abromowitz. You wouldn't think it would be that hard to remember."

"I can remember it," I said. I took a bite from

the meatballs and spaghetti I'd bought. Dina un-wrapped her sandwich. "Why didn't you get the spaghetti?" I asked her. "It's your favorite."

"I know," Dina said with a sigh. "But they don't use kosher meat. So I decided not to buy any of the meat lunches from now on. I got a tuna salad sandwich instead."

"They make horrible tuna salad," I said. "Are you sure you don't want some spaghetti?"

"Don't tempt me," Dina said. "It's hypocritical of me to eat kosher at home but not anywhere else. If I'm going to be kosher, I'm going to be kosher all the way." She took another bite. "Boy, do they make bad tuna salad," she said. "But I have to do what I think is right."

And that was when I realized the awful thing. Sure, it felt fine not to believe in God. That didn't bother me at all. But if I didn't believe in God, then how could I become a bat mitzvah?

I felt terrible. I had a mouthful of meatballs when I realized it, and I took all my power just to finish chewing and swallow. I didn't think I'd ever want to eat again. I pushed my plate away from me.

"I don't mind if you eat it," Dina said. "You're not keeping kosher, so it doesn't matter what you eat. Or do you think you want to keep kosher, too? It sure would be easier for me if you kept kosher. At least until the bat mitzvahs. What do you think?"

I wasn't thinking anything just then, my head felt so light. But I guess I said "sure," because Dina got excited.

"Do you mean it?" she asked. "You'll keep

kosher, too? That's so great, Becky. What an example we'll set for our families."

What had I just agreed to? If I'd decided there wasn't any God, what was the point of keeping kosher? What was the point of becoming a bat mitzvah? How could I stand there in front of my family and friends and congregation and Rabbi Greenberg and representing my Olga and declare my faith when I didn't have any?

But if Dina noticed my entire world had ended, she didn't say anything about it. "Have half of my tuna salad," she said, pushing the sandwich at me. "Do you want me to get back on line and buy you some milk? Now that you're having tuna, there's no reason why you can't drink some milk."

"Okay," I said. Anything to get her away from me. Dina smiled at me and got up. I sat there, stared at all the food I had no intention of eating, and tried to think.

Go ahead with the bat mitzvah, my brain told me. God won't care that you're lying because there isn't any God. And if you don't tell anyone that there isn't a God, then they won't care, either. It isn't like you'd be saying anything too untrue when you read from the Torah. It probably is best not to uncover Uncle Bob's nakedness. And even if you had to read the stuff about loving thy neighbor and leaving some grapes, you agree with it. It's good to love thy neighbor and to feed the poor. If you feel really bad about it, then keep your fingers crossed while you read.

And that was when I felt really sick. Dina came

back with the milk, but I just waved her away. "I feel awful," I said. "I'm going to the nurse."

"Do you want me to go with you?" she asked.

I shook my head.

"Do you think it's something serious?" she asked. "We have a bat mitzvah lesson tomorrow."

"I know," I said. "Maybe I'll be okay by then." I rose from my chair, and the whole room was spinning around. So I closed my eyes, took a deep breath, and when the room was standing still, I walked to the nurse's office.

"My stomach hurts," I told the nurse. "I want to go home."

The nurse looked at me. "You are pale," she said, and promptly rammed a thermometer in my mouth. I sat there sweating. But when she took it out, I didn't have a fever. "Have you been here before?" she asked me. "You don't look familiar."

"Never," I said. "I'm a very healthy person. But I feel awful."

"I'll call your mother," she said, so I gave her my mother's work number. Mom spoke to her, and then the nurse hung up. "She'll come pick you up," the nurse said. "And take you home."

I almost started crying, I was so happy to hear it. Instead, I waited with the nurse until Mom showed up. When she came, I went to my locker, got my jacket and books, and then she drove me home.

"I have to get back to work," Mom said. "Are you going to be okay by yourself?"

"I'll be fine," I said.

"Good," Dina said. "Then we can go to our bat mitzvah lesson together."

I thought I might throw up. But then I remembered about the clarinet, and I felt better instantly. "I can't," I said.

"Why not?" Dina asked. "Won't your mother let you?"

"No, it's me," I said. "I mean it's my clarinet. I had a lesson today, and I rescheduled it for tomorrow."

"Then call your teacher back and reschedule it again," Dina said. "Your bat mitzvah lesson is more important."

"I can't do that," I told her. "I already rescheduled it once. I can't keep calling my teacher. Besides, tomorrow was the only day she had free."

"Then skip a lesson," Dina said. "You're never going to be a great clarinet player, Becky. And our bat mitzvahs are less than five months away."

"No," I said, with more strength than I knew I had. "I'm sorry, Dina, but I'm going to have to miss my bat mitzvah lesson tomorrow. That's just how it is."

"Well, I don't understand," Dina grumbled.

She didn't, either. But I certainly wasn't going to explain it to her. Not until I'd figured things out better for myself.

Eight

Come on, Becky," Dina said to me Thursday after the last bell rang. "We don't want to be late for our lesson."

"I'm coming," I said and walked with her to our lockers. As we opened them, I looked at my watch, just the way I had rehearsed that morning, and said, "Oh, darn."

"Oh, darn, what?" Dina asked.

"I have to go home first," I said. "I promised my mother."

"What did you promise her?" Dina asked.

"That I'd go home first," I replied. It had sounded better that morning when I'd worked on it. "I have to turn the oven on for supper tonight."

"You do?" Dina said.

I nodded. "It'll only take a couple of minutes," I said. "I'll run. Tell Rabbi Greenberg not to worry about me."

"She's not the one worrying," Dina said, but I ignored her. I grabbed my books and my jacket and flew. I didn't know how I was going to explain to Dina that night that turning on the oven had taken an hour, but once I got home, I'd have plenty of time to work that one out. The important thing was to get away from her before going to our lesson. It was hard enough keeping kosher at lunchtime just to ward off questions.

As I was walking home, I spotted Amy trying to carry her books and a couple of paper bags. She wasn't doing too good a job of it. Mostly she was putting one bag down, or another, and sighing.

"Need help?" I asked her, after I caught up with her.

"Yeah," she said. "You, Becky?"

"The Bible says love thy neighbor as thyself," I informed her. "Leviticus, Chapter Nineteen. I'll take one bag and you take the other."

"Thanks," she said, handing me what was obviously the lighter of the two bags. "This is a big help."

"What's in the bags?" I asked her as we started walking toward her house.

"Stuff for my science project," Amy replied. "I'm doing a project on rocks."

"No wonder the bags are so heavy," I said.

"If it's too heavy for you, you don't have to carry it," Amy declared. "Let me take it. "

"Don't be dumb," I said. "I can manage."

"All right," she said.

We walked silently for half a block. "Besides," I

said, "this gives me a way to apologize to you."

"Apologize for what?" Amy asked, almost as though she didn't know.

"For the way I talked to you the other day," I said. "About Dina. About not liking you. I wasn't very nice."

"I shouldn't have asked you," Amy said.

I put her bag down for a moment and stared at her. "You drive me crazy, you know that," I said. "Why do you have to act like it's your fault when I'm rude?"

Amy stood there also. "I don't know," she finally said. "Can I think about that and get back to you?"

I laughed and Amy did also. It felt funny standing there laughing with her. I picked up the bag and we started walking again. "Dina still likes you," I said. "She's just wild about this bat mitzvah business."

"Well, I can understand that," Amy said.

"I don't think you can," I replied. "When Dina gets involved in something, she gets totally involved. It doesn't last too long usually, but it's a real nuisance while it does. Right now Dina's so involved with the bat mitzvah lessons, she wants to become a rabbi. I think she'd like me to become a rabbi, too. All she ever talks about is religion. You're better off waiting until she loses some of her interest and becomes a human being again."

"Thank you," Amy said. "Why didn't you just tell me that last week?"

I would have shrugged but the bag was too heavy. "Last week I was still nervous about you," I said.

"I need a volunteer to stay after school today and help me set up a display," she declared, practically the last thing that period. "It should only take a half hour or so. Are any of you free?"

My hand shot up so fast it startled even me. "I am!" I cried. "Pick me, Mrs. Maguire."

Mrs. Maguire looked like she was going to faint. "Are you sure, Becky?"

"Sure I'm sure," I said.

"Becky!" Dina screeched, but I ignored her and the last bell rang. Dina glared at me as she left the classroom, but I didn't care. I didn't even care that I had volunteered to spend half an hour with Mrs. Maguire. At least I was safe from another bat mitzvah lesson. Now all I needed was another thirty excuses or so and I was home free.

Mrs. Maguire and I worked quietly together, which was fine with me. It wasn't like I wanted to talk to her about anything, and I was afraid she'd bring up state capitals and make me recite them again, to see if I had retained them. I hadn't. The only one I ever remembered was Oklahoma City, Oklahoma, and that was because it was so easy.

When we finished putting the display together, I could see it was a giant three-dimensional map of the world with mountains and buildings and little people dressed in funny costumes.

"Our next project is world geography," Mrs. Maguire said. "You'll be the first one in our class to know that, Becky, because you were such a help."

"Thank you," I said, to show her what good

manners I had. Actually, I was thinking about how I was now going to have to learn the capitals of all the countries in the world. Maybe I could do that for the next four months instead of practicing reading the Torah.

I left Mrs. Maguire standing in front of her map, playing with some of the little funny-dressed people, and walked home slowly. I stopped everywhere I could think of between school and home, and did an awful lot of dawdling. I should have dawdled more, though. When I got to my house, I could see Dina standing there.

"Oh, hi," I said, nice and casual. "Do you want to come in?"

"Of course I want to!" she shrieked. I opened the door and we walked in together.

"What are you doing?" she demanded before I even had a chance to take my jacket off.

"Doing about what?" I asked.

"You've missed three lessons in a row!" Dina yelled. "I don't know what to tell Rabbi Greenberg. The first time it didn't make any sense, clarinet lessons instead, but okay. But then I had to say that you were going to be late because you had to turn the oven on, and then you don't show up at all. And today I said you were staying late to help Mrs. Maguire and you hate Mrs. Maguire and Rabbi Greenberg asked if she was the teacher with the state capitals and I said yes and even Rabbi Greenberg asked what was going on with you. And I had to say I didn't know, because I don't, but if it's what I think it is, I'm going to kill you."

"What do you think it is?" I asked. I didn't see how Dina could have figured out I didn't believe in God anymore, but she knows me awfully well.

"You always do this to me," Dina said instead. "We agree to do something together, and then you forget about things, or you're late, or you end up reading a book and not getting your work done. It's been like that since kindergarten and you're doing it again. I'll be all set to share our bat mitzvahs, and you'll probably forget to come, and I'll have to read all that stuff about uncovering nakedness and represent both Olgas and then you'll stroll in in time for the party and act like nothing's the matter. That's it, isn't it. I'll kill you if it is."

"That isn't it at all," I said. "And I always get the stuff done eventually."

"Eventually can take years," Dina replied. "What is it then? It had better be something really terrible in your life, or else you're dead meat."

I wondered if I'd be kosher dead meat, but I didn't ask. Instead, I cleared my throat.

"Out with it, Becky," Dina said.

"I will," I said. "This is hard."

"Being dead meat is going to be even harder," Dina said.

I licked my lips. "The thing is, I don't believe in God anymore," I said. The words sounded funny.

"What do you mean?" Dina asked. "How can you not believe in God?"

"I don't know," I said. "I just don't. So I don't see how I can become a bat mitzvah if I don't believe in God. You're the first person I've told."

"And the last, I hope," Dina said. "If you keep talking like that, God will strike you down dead."

"I don't think so," I said.

"Can't you lie?" Dina asked. "Tell everyone you believe in God, and go through with the bat mitzvah. Then you can tell people the truth, when it won't matter anymore."

"I'd really like to," I said. "But whenever I try to convince myself to do it that way, I get sick to my stomach. So I've been avoiding the lessons."

"I wouldn't mind if I wasn't doing it," Dina said. "I mean, I guess you won't become an ax murderer or anything because you don't believe in God. Will you?"

"I haven't believed in over a week," I said. "I think actually I've gotten nicer in the past week."

"Not to me, you haven't," Dina said, but she looked human again. She sat down on the sofa, and I sat there next to her. "I guess you'll have to tell your parents."

"I don't want to," I said.

"Then I will," Dina declared.

"You can't," I said. "That's tattling. And the Bible says you can't, remember? It's right there, in your chapter nineteen. You're not allowed to go up and down as a talebearer among thy people. And my parents are definitely thy people."

"You're cheating!" Dina said. "You can't say you don't believe in God and then quote Him to me, just to get your own way."

"So I'm cheating," I said. "I don't know what else to do. I haven't known for a week now. You think I like spending time with Mrs. Maguire? And I hate lying. Only if I tell Mom and Dad, they'll kill me. You still want to, don't you."

Dina nodded.

"I don't want to die for my faith," I declared. "Or even for my lack of faith. Especially not if my parents are the ones doing the killing."

"Someone's going to kill you," Dina said. "Me or your parents or Rabbi Greenberg. Take your pick."

"Can't we just let things slide?" I asked. "Only for the next four months or so. We can come up with lots of different excuses for Rabbi Greenberg, and my parents would never have to know."

"Yes they will," Danny said, walking into the living room. "Because if you don't tell them, I will."

"You've been listening," I said.

"You've been screaming," he replied. "Becky, you've got to tell Mom and Dad. They're planning to spend a lot of money on this bat mitzvah. If you aren't going to go through with it, you have to tell them now."

"I'm scared," I said.

"Come on," Danny said, and he sounded really nice. "How bad can it be?"

"Real bad," I said, and Dina nodded. But Danny was right, and I knew it. I had to tell Mom and Dad something, and the best story I could come up with was the truth.

Nine

Usually Danny left for school a few minutes after I did, but that next morning, he walked out with me. He wasn't the person I most wanted to talk to just then.

"You didn't say anything to Mom and Dad last night," he announced as we started walking toward our schools.

"How do you know?" I asked him.

"I would have heard," he replied. "Everyone in the galaxy would have heard."

"I wasn't ready to tell them," I said.

"You mean you were too scared to," Danny said.

"Of course I was scared!" I shouted. "You'd be scared, too, if you were me."

"I would never be you," Danny declared. "Not even under ordinary circumstances. But this one really takes the cake."

"I don't see how what I've done is so wrong," I

said. "I just don't believe in God anymore. Do you believe, Danny?"

"Of course I do," Danny replied. "Everybody does."

"I don't see how they all can," I said. "I mean, someone other than me must not. I'm not that smart that I'd be the first person to think this way."

"You're the first atheist I've ever met," Danny declared. "You're certainly the first one I've ever been related to."

"But haven't you ever had doubts?" I persisted. "Not even once?"

"Never," Danny said. "It's one of those things you're supposed to take for granted. Like who your parents are. You've never questioned that Mom and Dad are your parents, have you?"

"Well, yeah, I did once," I admitted. "A couple of years ago. I was sure I was adopted. You always knew they were your parents?"

"You're weird," Danny declared. "And you're getting weirder by the minute."

"I think it's strange not to question things," I said, wondering if I actually meant that. "There are so many things in this world that don't make sense. Like war and famines and teachers like Mrs. Maguire. I don't see how you can just accept stuff like that without asking questions."

"We're just kids," Danny replied. "Kids accept. Grown-ups question. And really old people know the answers. I heard that on TV once."

"Was it supposed to be a joke?" I asked.

"You're the joke," Danny said. "You're so sure

you're right, but you're scared to tell anyone. Especially Mom and Dad."

"Not just them," I said. "I'm scared to tell Rabbi Greenberg, too. I'm scared to tell lots of people."

"Once you tell Mom and Dad, the rest of the galaxy'll hear about it anyway," Danny declared. "So you might as well start with them. Today."

"You could tell them for me," I said.

"They kill the messenger with the bad news," Danny replied. "I'm not going to die just because you're weird."

"Just you wait," I said. "Someday you're going to want me to tell them something for you, and see if I do."

"See if I care," Danny said. "Tonight, Becky, or else." He turned off and started toward the high school.

I sighed and kept on walking. If Danny had been a perfect older brother, he would have told Mom and Dad for me, and calmed them down until we could all have a nice, rational conversation on the subject. Dad majored in philosophy in college, so he probably knew lots about people who didn't believe in God. Mom majored in economics, so I wasn't sure how much she'd know about belief, but she always had something interesting to say.

I imagined the four of us sitting around the dining room table, talking about God and religion, and then because I was enjoying the idea so much, I even had Rabbi Greenberg come in and talk with us also. It was a wonderful picture, and I figured it had as much of a chance to happen as my becoming Queen of England.

A couple of blocks from school I spotted Dina and Amy. That figured. Dina and I had been through a lot together, but I'd probably put one curse too many on our friendship.

"Hi," I said anyway.

"Hi, Becky," Amy said. "What happened after school yesterday?"

"What do you mean?" I asked.

"With Mrs. Maguire," Amy said. "What did the two of you do?"

"Oh, that," I said. "We set up a display of the world. It wasn't very much."

"The world sounds like a lot to me," Amy said, and then she giggled. Dina just glared.

"The world isn't very important to Becky right now," she declared. "She has bigger things on her mind."

"Like what?" Amy asked.

"Like telling her parents something," Dina said. "Did you, Becky?"

"Not yet," I said. "I will tonight."

"No you won't," Dina replied. "You never will. You'll just keep on making up excuses until it's too late."

"I will not!" I said. "I'm going to tell them tonight."

"Tell them what?" Amy asked. "What's Becky going to tell them that's bigger than the world?"

"Becky doesn't believe in God," Dina announced.

"She's an atheist. Just like Adolph Hitler."

"Adolph Hitler wasn't an atheist," I said. "He was a vegetarian. There's a difference."

"Well, then you're an atheist just like somebody else horrible," Dina said. "I'm sure there are lots of terrible atheists you can model yourself after."

"I'm not modeling myself after anybody," I said. "I just believe what I believe."

"You don't believe anything," Dina declared. "Atheists never do. Do they, Amy?"

"I don't know," Amy said. "I don't think I ever met an atheist before."

"What happens to atheists in your religion, Amy?" Dina asked. "Something terrible, I bet."

"I think they go to hell," Amy said. "But I've never really asked."

"Hear that, Becky?" Dina said. "You're going to go to hell."

"Only if I'm a Methodist," I said. "Which I'm not. No insult intended, Amy."

"That's okay," Amy said. "I hope you don't go to hell anyway."

"Me, too," I said. "Although it can't be much worse than staying after school with Mrs. Maguire."

"It's a lot worse," Dina declared. "I talked to Shawna Malloy about hell once. She's Catholic, so she really knows about it. Everybody burns there all the time, for all eternity. They scream from the pain and they're thirsty, too. There's no ice cream in hell, Becky, because it'd melt, and no TV, and all you do is burn and scream and everybody else there is just like Adolph Hitler. That's where you're going to go. Right, Amy?"

"Maybe," Amy said. "I'm really not sure. Besides, it isn't like Becky's going to die right now. She has lots of years to change her mind. You're still thinking about it, aren't you, Becky? You haven't absolutely decided yet, have you?"

"I think I have," I said, although I could have lived without burning next to Adolph Hitler for all eternity. That really didn't seem fair to me. "Anyway, I don't believe in hell. If there's no hell, then I don't have to worry about burning there. And once I'm dead, I'm not going to be eating ice cream anyway, Dina, or watching TV. Dead people don't eat ice cream. They get eaten by worms instead. Everybody knows that, don't they, Amy?"

"I don't know what it's like being dead," Amy replied. "I've never been dead. Do we have to keep talking like this?"

"See, Becky, you've bothered Amy," Dina said, and she put her arm around Amy to comfort her. "It's okay, Amy. We don't have to talk to this stupid atheist anymore."

"I am not stupid," I shouted. "I'm not weird, either."

"Yes you are," Dina said. "Why? Who told you you were?"

"Danny," I said.

"Well, he's right," Dina declared. "Which is pretty unusual for him. You don't know Danny, do you Amy? He always thinks he's right about things, but he never is. Except now. When he thinks Becky is weird and stupid."

"Not stupid," I said. "Just weird."

"I don't think Becky is stupid or weird," Amy declared, and for the first time since we'd met I actually kind of liked her. "I think maybe she's wrong, but that doesn't mean she's stupid or weird."

"You're just being nice," Dina said. "People who believe in God are always nice."

"People who don't believe can be nice, too," I said.

"They have to work harder at it," Dina said. "Because they can't count on God to help them."

That certainly was true. I hadn't thought much about not counting on God for the rest of my life. But then I remembered the state capitals and how I'd prayed like crazy and still hadn't known any of them except Albany.

"So I'll work harder at it," I said. "It seems to me you could work a little harder at it yourself, Dina. You're not being real nice to me right now."

"That's because you're weaseling out of the bat mitzvah," Dina declared. "And I hate you for that."

"You're not going to have your bat mitzvah?" Amy asked.

We both turned around to face her, she sounded so upset.

"How can she?" Dina asked. "Not believing in God?"

"I don't know," Amy said. "I just feel terrible about that. It sounded so interesting when you told me about it, Becky. And you really sounded excited about it all, like you cared and it interested you."

"I did," I said. "It did. I do."

"You do what?" Dina asked.

"I did want to become a bat mitzvah," I declared. "It did interest me and I did care."

"But not anymore, you don't," Dina said. "How can you, without God?"

"I don't know," I said.

"If God found a way for you, would you believe in God then?" Amy asked.

I hadn't been an atheist all that long, and I still wasn't sure of the ground rules. "I don't think I can believe in God no matter what happens," I told her. "I think it's an all-or-nothing kind of thing for me. And right now, it's nothing. But that doesn't mean I'm about to become a serial killer or anything. I'm still just me, only without God. That's all."

"Well, you were never very nice to me when you believed in God," Amy declared. "And you seem okay now. So maybe you know what's best for you, Becky. Just as long as you don't expect everybody else to stop believing."

I shook my head. "I don't care what anyone else believes," I said. "I just wish people would stop caring about what I believe in."

"That's not fair, Becky," Dina declared. "I wouldn't care if you worshipped rattlesnakes if we weren't supposed to share our bat mitzvahs. Which you got me into, since it was all your idea."

"I know," I said. "You're right about that, and I'm sorry."

"Sorry enough to tell your parents tonight?"

Dina asked. "So we can get this mess all straightened out before it's too late."

"I'll tell them," I said.

"Tonight?" she said.

"When the time is right," I said.

"Becky!" Dina shrieked, and then the strangest thing happened. It had been a cloudy day, and the weather report had predicted rain, but it was way past thunder and lightning season. Which didn't stop an enormous bolt of lightning from flashing across the sky, followed by a thunderclap loud enough to wake up the dead wherever they were.

All the kids started racing toward the school then, even though it hadn't started raining. There was a second bolt of lightning, and that only got us running faster.

"See," Dina said, as she and Amy and I ran to the door. "That's God talking to you, Becky."

"Don't be ridiculous," I said.

"I dare you to stand outside, then," Dina said. "And prove there isn't a God to strike you down dead."

"What if God did, Dina?" I said. "What if I stood outside and God struck me down dead just because of you? It'd be on your conscience then. You'd have to tell my parents it was all your fault I died. You want that, Dina? If you do, I'll go out there this very minute and stand under the biggest tree I can find and challenge God to strike me down dead because that's what you want for me, your best friend since before you were even born."

"Will you two stop it!" Amy cried. "Becky, get

inside this building right now, before it starts raining. Dina, stop talking about God striking people down dead."

It was amazing. The school was filled with kids, all of whom were screaming and yelling, and still Dina and I could hear every word Amy said, and Amy never talked above a whisper. We both stood there and stared at her.

"God or no God, you're both behaving very badly," Amy declared. "Dina, you know perfectly well you don't want Becky to die. And Becky, you know just as well you have to tell your parents what's going on. Tonight. No more excuses."

"Right, Amy," I said. "I promise I will. Tonight."

"It's your turn now, Dina," Amy said. "Tell Becky you don't think she should be stricken down dead, no matter what she believes in."

"I don't think you should be stricken down dead," Dina said. "But if you don't tell your parents tonight, and get this whole mess cleared up so that it won't hurt me, then I'm going to make my own lightning and you'll be sorry."

I was sorry already, with or without lightning. "I'll tell them tonight," I said again. "I absolutely promise."

"Good," Amy said. "And no more talk about worms. I just ate my breakfast, you know."

I thought I saw a little smile on Dina's face. I didn't push it, though. It was enough to think maybe she might smile at me again someday, if I could just say the right things to my parents to get the bat mitzvah business taken care of all right.

Ten

I have something I have to talk to you about," I informed my parents that evening. We had just finished supper, a meal I'd helped cook. I'd also set the table and brought Dad his slippers.

"Sure, honey," Mom said. "What's up?"

I looked at Danny, hoping he'd tell them for me, but he just scowled. It seemed extremely unfair to me that Leviticus Nineteen forbade tattletelling. Not that Mom or Dad were going to be any less furious if they learned the truth from somebody else.

"This is hard," I said, hoping they'd guess.

"Does it have something to do with school?" Dad asked. I sighed. You could always count on Dad to guess wrong.

"No," I said. "It has to do with me and the bat mitzvah. And God."

grade. Most people wait until high school, you know."

"Oh," I said. I hadn't known that at all.

"And what am I supposed to tell Bob?" Dad asked. "He asks about you every time we talk. He's been so proud of you. I think he figures today a bat mitzvah, tomorrow you move to Israel. I've been proud of you, too. And my parents! You've been the talk of Florida since I told them. And now they're going to have to learn the truth."

"I don't see why they have to, Hal," Mom said.

"How are we supposed to keep it from them?" Dad asked. "I'm going to call them up right now. Becky, get on the extension. I want you to hear their hearts breaking."

"Do I have to?" I asked.

"I think you'd better," Mom said. "This is no time to get Dad even more upset."

"Let me call them first," Dad said. He walked over to the kitchen phone and dialed the number. Only instead of saying "Hi," he was silent, and then he hung up.

"I don't believe this," he declared. "I got their machine. What was I supposed to say to it? Hi, this is your son, and your granddaughter is an atheist? What a thing for them to come home to."

"Hal, would you please calm down," Mom said. "When the time is right to tell them, we'll tell them."

"This bat mitzvah was all your idea," Dad said to me. "You were the one who pushed for it."

"We're listening," Mom said. That, of course, was what I was afraid of.

I swallowed hard. "The thing is," I began. "Well, you remember that day I forgot my math book?"

"No," Mom said.

"No, you wouldn't," I said. "I never told you about that. Well, it isn't important. It was the day I came home from school sick."

"Let me guess," Dad said. "When you were home alone, you had a vision."

"Hal!" Mom said.

"I'm serious," Dad said. "That happens a lot with prepubescent girls. Visions. Like Bernadette of Lourdes. If that's what's worrying you, Becky, don't let it. Unless, of course, your vision told you to turn our house into a shrine for the sick. I don't think we're zoned for that."

"Hal, stop talking and let Becky tell us what's bothering her," Mom said. I was sorry she did. I liked the idea of having had a vision. And I could see Dad would have enjoyed it, too. It was a shame Danny knew the truth, or else I could have said I'd had a vision not to become a bat mitzvah. But it was too late for creative lying.

"I didn't have a vision," I said. "At least not the kind you're talking about, Dad."

"What kind, then?" Dad asked.

"No kind," I said. "This is very hard to explain."

"Why don't you start from the beginning," Mom said. "And we'll all keep quiet so you can tell us your own way."

"It's just I forgot my math book," I said. "And I ran back to get it, and then after I left the house, I looked up at the sky, sort of like a vision, Dad, only instead of seeing something, I didn't." That didn't sound right at all. "Not like I was blind," I continued. "More like . . . well, what it comes down to is, I don't believe in God anymore."

"What?" Dad said.

"God," I said. "I've stopped believing. I looked up that day and it was like God wasn't there anymore. At least not for me."

"I don't believe this," Dad said. "You're twelve years old. People have been pondering the existence of God for centuries, more than that, thousands of years, and you're going to sit here at our dining room table and announce you know the one true answer?"

"No," I said. "I mean, I don't know. It's just that I don't believe anymore. Do you want me to lie about it?"

"Of course not," Mom said. "It must have been very difficult for you, Becky, to stop believing like that."

If I wasn't going to lie, then I wasn't going to lie. "Not exactly," I said. "Actually, it felt okay. You know. Like when something is bothering you and you can't figure out the answer, and then all of a sudden it comes to you. It was like that. I wouldn't mind at all not believing, except for the bat mitzvah."

"The bat mitzvah," Dad said, and then he turned

to Danny. "And how long have you known a this?" he asked. When Dad's mad, he likes to bl things on everybody.

"Just since yesterday," Danny said. "I'm the who insisted Becky tell you."

"Dina knows, too," I said. "I told her she could tell you because of Leviticus Nineteen. It says the you can't go up and down as a talebearer amo thy people. But Danny heard what we were sayin and he said I had to tell you. Because of the ba mitzvah and what it was going to cost."

"Thank you, Danny," Mom said. Dad still looked too angry to thank anybody.

"I think she's crazy," Danny said. "I believe in God."

I tried kicking him under the table but my leg was too short.

"I don't know how I can go through with the bat mitzvah if I don't believe in God," I said.

"Hold on one second, young lady," Dad said. "Have you stopped believing in God, or do you just want to get out of this bat mitzvah? Are the lessons too much for you? Is that what's going on here?"

"The lessons aren't too much," I said. "Besides, I haven't been going lately. That's why Dina got so upset. I've missed my last three lessons. But before then I was having a good time. I liked the lessons. I like Rabbi Greenberg."

"She's twelve years old and she doesn't believe in God," Dad declared. "She's an atheist in seventh

"I know," I said, hoping he wouldn't question my motives. Telling him about God was bad enough. If he heard about Amy as well, I'd be in real trouble.

"Can I ask a question?" Danny said.

"Sure," Dad said. "What's another question at this dinner table?"

"I was just wondering if you were mad at Becky because she doesn't believe in God anymore, or because of the bat mitzvah," Danny said.

"That's a very good question," Mom said. "And come to think of it, we don't know what Becky wants to do about the bat mitzvah."

"Not go through with it," I said, and my stomach hurt all over again. I hadn't realized until I actually said it how much I was going to miss becoming a bat mitzvah. I'd enjoyed the lessons and asking Rabbi Greenberg questions and learning about being a Jew. And now I was going to have to give all that up because I didn't believe in God. Not to mention having Dad mad at me at least until I went off to college.

Mom nodded. "I'm glad that's been clarified," she said. "Now, Hal, what is making you angry?"

"All of this," Dad said, but he started looking thoughtful.

"All of this what?" Mom asked.

Dad pushed his plate away. "I'm disappointed," he admitted. "I was looking forward to the bat mitzvah. I liked the way Becky was learning so much about Judaism. I know I don't go to temple often enough, and I'm not a religious man, but I liked the idea that Becky had made a commitment to the faith. I guess it was all your arguments, Annie, yours and Sharon's. I don't know. I even had fantasies that Becky might end up becoming a rabbi. To my father, there's no one more important than a rabbi. It's better even than being a doctor. I guess I believe some of that, too. I feel let down."

"I'm sorry, Dad," I said. "I never meant to stop believing. It just happened."

Dad looked straight at me. "You have every right to believe or disbelieve," he declared. "That's in the Constitution. No one, not even me, can force you to believe in God. Don't you ever forget that."

"I won't," I said. "And Dad, even when I did believe, I didn't plan on being a rabbi. Dina's talking about it, but not me. I want to be a lawyer, like you."

Dad grinned. "You may not believe in God anymore, but you sure know how to make a man feel guilty," he declared. "Some aspects of the faith you never lose."

"I thought you wanted to be a clarinet player," Danny said.

"That was last year," I replied. "Not anymore."

"It's nice that you want to be a lawyer," Mom said. "And I'm certainly pleased your father realizes you can believe in anything you want, but we still have a problem."

"We do?" I said.

"We do," Mom said. "What are we going to do about your bat mitzvah?"

"Not have it," I said. "Dina already knows, so she can do whatever she wants. You can tell Rabbi Greenberg, and she can tell my Olga. Dina can tell hers. Dad can tell his parents and Uncle Bob, and that takes care of everybody."

"It's not that simple," Mom declared. "If you're old enough to question your faith, then you're old enough to live with the consequences."

"But I am living with the consequences," I replied. "I told you. And before that I told Dina. And I know I won't have a big party and get all those presents. What other consequences are there?" I was afraid Mom might think God was going to strike me down dead, but I figured I was better off not mentioning it unless she did.

Mom stared me straight in the eye. All of a sudden I realized I was happier when Dad was running around calling his parents to break their hearts. At least they weren't home. I definitely was.

"We're not going to tell Rabbi Greenberg a thing," Mom declared.

"That's great," I said. "You mean I should just keep coming up with excuses to miss my lessons? I can do that. Especially if you'll help me. Maybe we could say Danny was sick, and I have to spend all my time at the hospital. Or I could just change the days of my clarinet lessons. I don't want to be a clarinet player anymore, but Rabbi Greenberg doesn't have to know that."

"We are not going to come up with ridiculous excuses for you," Mom said. "If you honestly don't believe in God and feel that you can't go through with the bat mitzvah, you'll tell Rabbi Greenberg yourself."

"But what am I supposed to say?" I asked.

"Tell her what you told us," Mom said, and for the first time I could see how angry she was. "Tell her you looked at the sky and found there was no God. Tell her you're turning your back on thousands of years of tradition and values. Tell her you're rejecting a faith millions upon millions of people have died for rather than renounce. Tell her you're giving up your right, your privilege to be a member of the oldest religion still being practiced on earth. Tell her whatever you want. You're old enough to have opinions, you're old enough to live with the consequences."

"That's not what I want," I said, no longer sure what it was I did want. "I don't want to tell her all that."

"Tell her something else, then," Mom said with a sigh. "Just as long as it's the truth. You owe Rabbi Greenberg that. Now, if you'll excuse me, I seem to have gotten a headache." She stood up and walked away from the table.

I stared at Dad and Danny. "Why is it so bad?" I asked them. "To believe what I want to believe."

Dad frowned. "It's never easy to be in the minority," he said. "It's always easier to go with the crowd. Now, if you'll excuse me, I think I'd better talk with your mother and see if I can calm her down."

I nodded. It definitely was easier to go with the crowd. Especially when the crowd was your parents and brother and friends and rabbi. I wished I could be angry at them and think that they were wrong. I wished I could change my beliefs and agree with them so there'd be no problems. At that moment, I almost wished the bolt of lightning had struck me down dead when it had the chance.

Eleven

I knocked on Rabbi Greenberg's door and hoped she wouldn't be in. I knew she would be, since it was my usual time to have a lesson with her and Dina. Only Dina wasn't with me, and instead of a lesson, I had to tell the rabbi all about how I didn't believe in God anymore. This was just the kind of situation I used to pray in, and now I couldn't even do that. It was hard being an atheist.

"Come in," Rabbi Greenberg said. "Oh, hi, Becky. Where's Dina?"

"She isn't coming today," I said. "I have to talk to you about something. Dina knows what it's all about, and so do my parents, and now I have to tell you." I walked into the office and looked at the pictures of the Israeli children. I wished I were in Israel with them.

"It sounds mysterious," Rabbi Greenberg said

with a smile. "Is there anything I can do to help?"
She didn't have to be that nice, especially since I'd
been cutting classes for the past ten days.

"I don't know," I admitted. I sat down in the
chair facing her desk. Rabbi Greenberg had been
going through some papers, but she pushed them
aside and smiled at me again. I wondered if she'd
end up as mad as Mom.

"I know something's wrong," she said. "Do you
want to tell me what's been bothering you?"

"No," I said. "But my mother says I have to."

Rabbi Greenberg laughed. "My mother says I
have to do things all the time," she said. "I imagine
when I'm a mother I'll order my kids around, too."

"Do you think you'll have kids soon?" I asked.

"Soon enough," Rabbi Greenberg replied. "But
that's not why you've come to see me."

"No," I said. "My father says I have the right to
believe in whatever I want. He says it's in the
Constitution."

"It sure is," Rabbi Greenberg said. "That's one
reason why Jews are so proud to be Americans.
It's a country that encourages people to hold onto
their beliefs."

"Or give them up," I said.

Rabbi Greenberg breathed deeply. "Becky, you're
confusing me," she declared. "If you'll tell me
what's the matter, maybe we can figure out how
to deal with it together."

"Probably not," I told her. "The thing is, I don't
believe in God anymore."

"Oh?" Rabbi Greenberg said. She put a lot into that "oh."

"Yeah," I said, nodding sadly. "I didn't mean for it to happen. It just did."

"So you didn't think about it," Rabbi Greenberg said. "You didn't make lists or try to prove or disprove anything."

"I looked up at the sky and God wasn't there anymore," I said. "Are you mad?"

"I don't know," Rabbi Greenberg replied. "Are your parents?"

"First Dad was hysterical," I said. "Because of his family. And then Mom got really angry because she said I was renouncing my faith. She hardly talked to me this morning, she was still so mad. It was awful."

"It sounds it," Rabbi Greenberg replied. "Oh, Becky, you are a complicated girl."

"I am?" I said.

Rabbi Greenberg nodded. "If you didn't believe in God, why did you decide to become a bat mitzvah?"

"I believed then," I said. "I prayed to Him all the time, not that it did me much good."

"So you decided to become a bat mitzvah because of your religious beliefs," Rabbi Greenberg said.

I shook my head and looked away from her. "The bat mitzvah was so Dina and I would stay best friends," I said. "She was getting too friendly with Amy Ford, and she's a Methodist, so I thought we could study for our bat mitzvahs together, and Amy wouldn't be able to join us."

"Oh, Becky," Rabbi Greenberg said. "Now I am mad."

"Do you want me to leave?" I asked.

"I want you to be honest with me," Rabbi Greenberg declared. "Which I gather you haven't been for months now."

I felt worse than I ever did when Mrs. Maguire was mad at me. I didn't care if Mrs. Maguire didn't like me, but Rabbi Greenberg was someone I respected. I wanted her to like me, and now she never was going to again.

Rabbi Greenberg looked at me and sighed. Then she glanced at all those papers she'd pushed away from her and sighed some more.

"Do you think you'll still have kids?" I asked her.

"Becky!" she said.

"I wouldn't want to think you decided not to because of me," I told her. "I have enough I feel bad about, as it is."

"I'm not going to laugh," Rabbi Greenberg declared. "And I'm not going to scream, either. What I'm going to do is get us both a glass of water. I'm taking mine with aspirin."

"Okay," I said. I seemed to be giving people headaches lately. The Israeli kids in the pictures all seemed to have gotten headaches, too.

Rabbi Greenberg came back a minute or two later carrying two paper cups of water. She popped a couple of aspirin and swallowed half her cup of water. I drank mine as well.

"All right," she said, and she sat down on the

chair next to mine so there wouldn't be a desk separating us. "Now, let's really talk."

"About what?" I asked. I figured since I'd told her the worst, there was nothing else to say.

"About you," Rabbi Greenberg replied. "About your bat mitzvah lessons. About what Judaism means to you."

"That's a lot," I said.

"It sure is," she replied. "Let's start with the lessons. I was under the impression you were enjoying them."

"I was," I said. "I hated missing them. But I didn't see how I could keep going to them when I didn't believe in God anymore."

"I could see how you might feel that way," Rabbi Greenberg declared. "But I wish you'd been honest with me from the beginning."

"I wish I had, too," I said. "Dina and Amy both think I'm going to go to hell. And Shawna Malloy says hell is a horrible place where I'll burn for all eternity with Adolph Hilter."

"Who's Shawna Malloy?" Rabbi Greenberg asked.

"Just someone in my class," I replied.

"Then let's leave her out of this, all right?" Rabbi Greenberg said. "I don't want my headache to get worse."

"Do you think I'm going to go to hell?" I asked.

"No," Rabbi Greenberg said. "I truly don't."

"Good," I said. "Things are bad enough as it is without having that to look forward to."

Rabbi Greenberg laughed. "I'm feeling better.

116

Maybe it was the aspirin. Or maybe hell put things in perspective."

"I'm glad," I said. "I didn't mean to stop believing in God. Honest."

"I know," she said. "Nobody chooses to believe things that are going to cause problems."

"There's no problem anymore," I replied. "Except maybe with my mother. Now that you know the truth, you'll just say I shouldn't become a bat mitzvah and I'll forget about everything."

"Is that what you want?" Rabbi Greenberg asked.

I thought about it and didn't know what to reply.

"Let me ask you another question," Rabbi Greenberg said. "And I want you to really think about your answer. You admitted your reasons for becoming a bat mitzvah weren't good ones. You did it to manipulate Dina, and that was dishonest if not cruel. You do know that, don't you?"

I nodded "It was dishonest and I was wrong," I admitted. "And I've been worrying about it."

"Then, here's my question," Rabbi Greenberg said. "Do you think you stopped believing in God because you were feeling bad about what you did to Dina?"

That was a very good question. I remembered that day, going back for my math book and looking up at the sky. I was feeling bad about how I'd treated Amy, and maybe that meant I felt bad about Dina as well.

But not believing in God had felt so right to me. It didn't make me feel good or bad, just natural.

And I couldn't believe that something that had felt so natural would have happened just because I felt bad about something I didn't feel all that bad about. I'd known all along Dina would enjoy the lessons once she got interested.

I looked at the Israeli kids, and they didn't look like they had headaches anymore. They just seemed interested.

"No," I said. "Dina wasn't why. It was more those questions we talked about, why God lets bad things happen. If there isn't a God, then naturally bad things will happen. There's nobody to stop them except people. But if you don't believe in God, you don't have to keep making excuses for Him."

"I don't make excuses for God," Rabbi Greenberg declared. "We talked about reasons for things we can't understand. We talked about faith."

"Okay," I said. "You can believe in God. The whole world can. I just don't."

Rabbi Greenberg stared at me and then drank the rest of her water. "Do you still want to be a Jew?" she asked.

"Sure," I said. "Can I be?"

She nodded.

"Oh, good," I said. "Mom really got me upset about that. I never wanted to renounce being a Jew. But she made me think that since I stopped believing in God, that meant I couldn't be anything anymore."

"It doesn't work that way," Rabbi Greenberg declared. "Being a Jew involves a lot more than believing in God. There are rules of conduct, ways you should behave."

"Like Leviticus?" I asked. "Not being a talebearer and loving thy neighbor and not uncovering your uncle's nakedness?"

"There's more to it than Leviticus," Rabbi Greenberg replied. "But that's good for a start."

"What else is there?" I asked.

Rabbi Greenberg rubbed the back of her neck. "Remember when we talked about Jews being part of a family?" she asked.

"Sure," I said.

"You don't stop being a member of a family just because you disagree with them," Rabbi Greenberg said. "My father and I have had terrible fights, but he's still my father and I'm still his daughter. We'll always love each other. We'll always be family."

"So I'm still part of the Jewish family," I said.

"You will be forever," Rabbi Greenberg replied. "And you can be a good Jew, too, even if you don't believe in God."

"As good as my uncle Bob?" I asked.

"You can certainly try," Rabbi Greenberg declared. "If you want to."

"I do," I said.

"And you're not saying that because you want to make me happy," Rabbi Greenberg said. "Or your parents. Or to make Dina like you."

"I like being a Jew," I replied. "I really liked the bat mitzvah lessons."

"I thought you did," Rabbi Greenberg said. "Would you like to continue them?"

"Not if I can't become a bat mitzvah," I told her.

Rabbi Greenberg laughed. "Let me ask you something else," she said. "Suppose you could become a bat mitzvah, but there'd be no party, no celebration. Do you still think you'd want to go through with it?"

Rabbi Greenberg asked harder questions than Mrs. Maguire ever dreamed of. "Would I get gifts?" I asked.

"No gifts," she replied.

"Then why would I become one?" I asked.

"To show you want to be a member of the community," she declared. "To show that you're old enough to be respected and to have your beliefs respected."

"Then sure," I said. "The community is being Jewish, right? And I like being Jewish. And I want people to respect my beliefs. They don't have to agree with me, but I don't want them to say I can't believe in something because I'm just a kid."

"Fair enough," Rabbi Greenberg said. "If you really feel that way, then I don't see why you can't become a bat mitzvah."

"Even without God?" I asked.

"Even without God," Rabbi Greenberg declared. "Frankly, I'd rather help someone become a bat mitzvah who knows there are questions and asks them and works out answers for herself. Most kids come in here and they do it for the party and because their parents expect them to and because they've been brought up believing that a bat mitzvah is something you do when you're thirteen and they don't even think about it. I don't agree with you. I believe in God, a loving, caring God. But I certainly respect you for thinking about it, for caring enough to think about it. It would be a pleasure to share in your bat mitzvah."

"Can I still be twinned with my Olga?" I asked.

"You certainly can," Rabbi Greenberg replied. "She lives in a country where you're not supposed to believe in God. I'm sure she'd understand your doubts. She'd probably envy you your choices."

The way I'd been feeling she had nothing to envy. "Thank you," I said, starting to get up. "Can I come to my regular lesson next Tuesday?"

"I'm looking forward to it," Rabbi Greenberg said, and when she smiled, I knew she meant it.

"And can Dina still have a party?" I asked. "Even if I can't?"

"As far as I'm concerned, you can both have a party," Rabbi Greenberg said. "What do you think, there's a law that says atheists can't have bat mitzvah parties?"

"But you said—"

"I asked if you'd still want to become a bat mitzvah even if you couldn't have a party," Rabbi Greenberg declared. "And you said you would. So I imagine you'd really like to become one with a party to look forward to as well."

"I don't know how my parents are going to feel," I said.

"I'll give them a call tonight, and we'll talk it all out," Rabbi Greenberg replied. "Have a little faith, Becky."

"I'll try," I said. "If they say it's okay, will you come to the party?"

"Are you kidding?" she said. "I wouldn't miss it for the world."

I couldn't blame her. I wouldn't miss it for the world, myself.

Twelve

It was the best bat mitzvah an atheist could have dreamed of.

Of course, I was nervous before the service actually began. Mom and Dad and even Danny kept encouraging me, telling me how great I'd do and how proud they were of me, but I kept picturing everything that might go wrong. I could forget all the Hebrew I knew, forget just how to read the Torah, forget which Olga was mine. By the time we walked to the temple, I had practically forgotten my own name.

But once the service began, the terror became just plain nervousness, and that I could handle. Dina and I sat in front of the congregation, and there were two empty seats besides us, each with one of the Olga's names on it. I looked at my Olga a lot while I was waiting to be called to the Torah. At Rabbi Greenberg's suggestion, we'd started corresponding with our Olgas, and soon they weren't just names. They became real people, girls our own age, who were proud to be Jewish, just the way we were, but couldn't celebrate their religion, something Dina and I took for granted. Dina and I had talked a lot about our Olgas the past few months, and we'd agreed we'd keep writing to them. Maybe someday we'd even go to the Soviet Union and meet them.

And then I was called to the Torah. I walked up alone, my knees knocking, my stomach churning, and I was convinced I'd forget everything. But the words were so familiar to me, I had them memorized by then, and soon I was reciting Leviticus Eighteen, my Leviticus Eighteen, all full of nakedness and beasts. I didn't care if anyone else knew what I was reading. I didn't care that I didn't get to read about loving thy neighbor. I was reading from the Torah, the same as millions of Jews had done for thousands of years. I was part of something so big I couldn't even picture it, and I loved it.

Dina read Leviticus Nineteen, starting with a slightly shaky voice, but then getting more and more confident as she went along. When the time came, we read our Haftorah portions as well.

We even got to give short speeches. Dina's was about our two Olgas, and how sharing our bat mitzvahs helped us understand each other, even though we live thousands of miles away.

I knew Mom and Dad were real nervous about my speech, which I'd refused to show them. But I could see they were pleased when I talked about how coming of age meant not only asking questions, but listening to and respecting other people's answers. "When a mother respects a daughter, then the daughter is old enough to become a bat mitzvah," I said. "But when a daughter respects her mother, then the daughter is worthy to become one." Mom loved it.

Rabbi Greenberg gave a wonderful sermon. It was all about youth and questions and not being satisfied with easy answers. "Leviticus Nineteen tells us to love our neighbors as we love ourselves," she declared. "And that means accepting them, whether we agree with their beliefs or not." I knew she was talking about me, even if hardly anybody else in temple did. I looked around at all the people there, my parents first, and Danny, then Dina's parents. They were beaming. I think I was, too.

And I looked at the other people there, sharing our moment. Amy had come with a bunch of our friends from school, and while I know she couldn't have understood a word that we'd read, and that our prayers might have seemed strange to her, she followed what we were doing, and she listened carefully to Rabbi Greenberg's sermon. That, at least, was in English.

And Uncle Bob was there as well, even though our temple wasn't nearly religious enough for his taste. He came with Judy, who wasn't his girlfriend anymore, since they'd gotten married two months earlier. It had been exciting going to their wedding and getting a new aunt. Even Dad liked Judy, although he still grumbled occasionally about not being able to play tennis with Bob on Saturdays.

And sitting by herself toward the back was Mrs. Maguire. I don't know why I invited her, except maybe to show her just how much I could memorize if I wanted to, and because sometimes I felt if I had bothered to learn all the state capitals in the first place, I might never have become a bat mitzvah. But she was there, along with some other teachers Dina and I had. It made me feel even prouder to see them there.

But looking proudest of all were my grandparents. They'd given up their favorite Friday night TV shows to come to New York, and they sat with Mom and Dad, and their smiles were so bright you could have read a book by them. Every time I looked at them, I smiled, too, so after a while I tried not to look there. A bat mitzvah was a solemn occasion, and I didn't want people to think I was grinning at a joke or something.

When the service ended, I joined my family, and the hugging began. There was so much of it, I thought I'd never be able to breathe again. There was also a lot of kissing, and a fair amount of teary eyes and blowing noses. I loved it. Nobody cried when Danny became a bar mitzvah.

"Today you are a woman," Dad kept saying, which I'd always thought had something to do with when you got your first period, but I guess religion was involved, too. "Just yesterday, it seems, you were a baby, and now today you are a woman."

"You're still just my kid sister," Danny growled, but he was grinning, and even he kissed and hugged me and said he was proud. "You read almost as well as I did," he said. "You may have stumbled less, but I had more feeling."

"You can't have feeling when you're reading about nakedness," I told him.

"Nakedness?" Grandma said.

"That's what my Torah portion was about," I told her. "How you shouldn't uncover people's nakedness. There wasn't anything in there about not uncovering grandparents' nakedness, but pretty much everybody else was included. Also, how you shouldn't lie down with beasts."

"I should hope not," Grandma said. "I'm glad I didn't know what you were reading. I would have been so embarrassed."

"That's why I had to read it," I said. "Dina was too embarrassed to. She read about loving thy neighbor as thyself instead."

"She did a very good job, too," Grandma declared. "But you had the harder portion to read, since it was full of such embarrassing things. You should be doubly proud of yourself."

I love Grandma. To show her I did, I gave her a big kiss. That was when the handkerchiefs started making their appearances.

In addition to the big party that was scheduled for Sunday afternoon, Dina's parents and mine gave us a kiddush at the temple. Everybody who'd been at the service was invited. We all said the blessing over the wine, drank it, and ate the sponge cakes and honey cakes and celebrated not just our bat mitzvahs, but the Sabbath as well.

"I couldn't get over the two of you," Dina's father declared as we stood around the table. Dina was standing next to him, looking about ten feet tall. I felt like I could look her straight in the eye, though, so I guess I'd grown pretty tall, too. "You've both worked hard these past months, and it really showed. I'm sorry my father couldn't have been here to see you. He would have been impressed."

"I'm not sorry," Dina's mother declared. "It's always so much easier when just one of them shows up."

"The way they've worked it, Granny came today, and Granddad's coming tomorrow," Dina said.

"You know, that's the first thing they've agreed on in over twenty years," Ted said. "Maybe this bat mitzvah is the start of a whole new era in my family's relations."

"Isn't faith wonderful?" Sharon said. "Come on, Ted. You'd better start making more of a fuss over your mother, or else she'll decide your father's getting the better of the deal."

So Dina and I stood alone for a moment, and then Amy walked over to us. "I thought you were wonderful," she said. "I mean, I don't know any Hebrew, so I couldn't be sure you were doing what you were supposed to be doing, but you seemed like you must be, so I figured you were. If that makes any sense."

"It makes lots of sense," I told her. "And we did know what we were doing."

"It was awfully nice of you to come," Dina

declared. "I know there was a horse show you were supposed to compete in today."

"This was more important," Amy replied. "I felt like a part of all this."

"You are," I said, and it was wonderful to say it. "You were a big part, Amy, and it wouldn't have seemed right if you hadn't been here to share it with us."

"I wish I could share your presents, too," Amy said, and she giggled. She'd been doing more and more of that lately around us, saying funny things and laughing. She wasn't quite as polite as she used to be, either. I liked her a lot more than I ever would have thought possible.

"We'll be getting most of our gifts tomorrow," Dina said. "At the party."

"Don't forget to bring some canned goods," I said. "We're going to drive them over to the soup kitchen with Rabbi Greenberg after school on Monday. I want us to have lots of food to donate."

"I already reminded my mother," Amy said. "She says she'll give me a whole bag's worth to bring."

"Great," I said, but before I had a chance to thank her, Mrs. Maguire had marched over to us.

"That was a very impressive service, girls," she declared. "You made all of us in your social studies class quite proud."

"Thank you," we muttered.

"It simply proves what you can do if you put your mind to it," she said. "Especially you, Becky. I hope you'll use some of that fine memory and willingness to work with our next area of study."

"What's that?" I asked.

"We are going to learn the names of all the rivers of the world," Mrs. Maguire said. "Their location and size. We start on Monday."

"I can hardly wait," I told her. I thought Dina was going to burst, she was trying so hard not to laugh. But while Amy had been losing some of her manners, I'd been working on becoming more polite. Mrs. Maguire was never going to think I was rude again.

"Very good, girls," she said, and then she took a glass of wine. That was when I thought I'd die. Luckily, she crossed the room before I collapsed with giggles.

"You look very happy," Uncle Bob said. He was holding hands with Judy, who kept smiling at him. They'd been that way since they got married. Mom said she and Dad were that way, too, the first couple of months after they got married. "It goes fast enough," she said. "Let them enjoy it while they can."

"I am happy," I told him.

"You read the Torah beautifully," Judy said. "The synagogue we're members of doesn't allow women to read the Torah. Up until today, I never minded, but hearing your voices, and seeing your rabbi, made me think I might prefer to belong to a temple that encourages its women to be more a part of the service."

"I think that's a wonderful idea," I said. If Bob and Judy joined our temple, there was a chance

Bob would start playing tennis on Saturdays again.

"I'm thinking of becoming a rabbi," Dina declared. "Or a veterinarian." Last week she'd seen a dog get hit by a car, and ever since then all she'd talked about was helping injured animals. I figured I was in for six months of talk about the needs of dogs and cats, but that was okay, too.

"Girls, I'd like you to meet my husband," Rabbi Greenberg said. "Hank, these are Dina and Becky, who I've told you so much about."

"It's nice to meet you, Dr. Greenberg," Dina said.

"Dr. Schwartz," he said. "Hank Schwartz."

"Oh, I'm sorry," Dina said.

"Nothing to be sorry about," he said. "When I take Liz places, people always assume her name is Schwartz. We're used to it by now."

I checked Dr. Schwartz out. He was tall and had dark curly hair, and when he smiled, he had dimples. He looked pretty close to perfect, so I guessed he was good enough for our Rabbi Greenberg. Instead of telling him that, though, I smiled. I guess he knew what my smile meant, because he smiled right back.

The kiddush didn't last long, but I enjoyed every moment of it. People kept congratulating us. A lot of them I knew from going to temple every week. It was funny. Ever since I stopped believing in God, I'd gotten a lot more religious. And I loved sharing this day with them. It was like being part of a big family, and I knew they were proud of me just the way family members are.

131

"I don't know about you," Dina whispered to me when things were almost over. "But I've got to pee."

"Me, too," I said. We ran to the ladies' room and did. While Dina was washing her hands, I figured I ought to tell her the one thing I'd been avoiding for the past six months.

"There's something I've got to say," I began.

Dina turned the water off. "You've decided to become a Catholic," she said.

"No," I said, but I grinned. "I'm still a Jewish atheist. I think I will be for a while yet."

"Then what do you have to say?" she asked. She took a paper towel and dried her hands with it.

"It's about why I started this whole bat mitzvah business," I said. "I've been scared to tell you all this time because I was afraid you might drop out."

"You started it because you were jealous of Amy and you wanted something we could do just by ourselves," Dina said. "Right?"

I nodded. "That's it exactly," I said. "How long have you known?"

"Since you first came up with the idea," Dina replied. "Becky, when you've been best friends with someone since forever, you know why they do things."

"Oh," I said. "I mean, I know why you do things, but I never thought you knew why I did things, too."

"Of course I do," Dina declared. "You're not a real subtle person, Becky. Surprising sometimes, but not subtle."

"Well, you're pretty obvious sometimes yourself," I said. "At least you are to me."

Dina grinned. "We're more than friends," she said. "We both know that. But that means that we can be friends with other people, and it shouldn't make any difference to us. Sometimes I like doing things with other kids. You do, too. And you can drive me crazy more than anybody else I know. But that's because you're more than my friend. You're the only sister I've ever had."

"Oh, Dina," I said.

"That's assuming my parents don't do something dumb, like have a baby," she said. "They've been making goo-goo eyes at each other lately. I'm not sure I like it."

"Do you really think they might have a baby?" I asked. It seemed like such a strange thing for parents to do.

"I sure hope not," Dina declared. "But if they do, I'm going to get a dog. Maybe two. And a cat. That'll show 'em."

"Have you forgotten already?" I asked. "You're supposed to love thy neighbor as thyself."

"That's neighbor, not parent," Dina said. "Besides, there's nothing in the Bible that says you can't have a pet. Just as long as you don't lie down with it."

"I won't if you won't," I promised.

"That's a deal," Dina said, and with both of us laughing, we walked back to our families together.

About the Author

SUSAN BETH PFEFFER is the author of many popular books for young readers, among them *Starting with Melodie, Truth or Dare, The Friendship Pact,* and *The Year Without Michael,* recently named an ALA Best Book for Young Adults.

She lives and works in Middletown, New York.

Temple Israel

Minneapolis, Minnesota

IN HONOR OF
THE 88TH BIRTHDAY OF

ROSE SCHLEIFF